THE BEST FRIEND'S
BILLIONAIRE BROTHER

BREE LIVINGSTON

Edited by
CHRISTINA SCHRUNK

The Best Friend's Billionaire Brother

Copyright © 2018 by **Bree Livingston**

Edited by Christina Schrunk

https://www.facebook.com/christinaschrunk.editor

Proofread by Krista R. Burdine

https://www.facebook.com/iamgrammaresque

Cover design by Victorine Lieske

http://victorinelieske.com/

Bree Livingston

https://www.breelivingston.com

Publisher's Note: This is a work of fiction. Names, characters, places, and incidents are a product of the author's imagination. Locales and public names are sometimes used for atmospheric purposes. Any resemblance to actual people, living or dead, or to businesses, companies, events, institutions, or locales is completely coincidental.

The Best Friend's Billionaire Brother/ Bree Livingston. --
1st ed.

ISBN: 9781691228638

To my oldest child. Be weird, baby, be weird. Normal never changed the world. One day, you will.

CHAPTER 1

*G*abby Fredericks waited at one of the cubicles closest to her new editor-in-chief's office for her end-of-the-day meeting with him. Any minute, she was going to be called back, and she was already practicing how she would accept the promotion from section editor to copy editor. Changes were coming to the Charleston Uptown Gazette, and she wanted to be the first on board with modernizing the newspaper.

"Ms. Fredericks," Wesley Brown finally called. He'd been the first change the publisher made. The previous editor-in-chief of the paper had wanted to retire, and when they were bought out, he decided it was the best time to leave.

She stood and crossed the newsroom floor, shaking hands with him as she reached his office. "Hi."

"Come on in." He stepped aside, allowing her in, and she noticed a woman behind Wesley's desk.

Instead of being her normally meek self, she walked right over and shook the woman's hand. "Hi, I'm Gabby Fredericks."

The woman waved to the chair across from her. "Please, take a seat."

Gabby complied and set her hands in her lap. "I'm so—"

"Ms. Fredericks, before we get too chummy, I'm here to let you know that Wayne Publishing has decided to go a different direction with producing this paper."

"Okay," Gabby said softly, unconsciously rubbing the office key on her wristlet.

"With that said, we're letting you know that today is your last day." The woman slid an envelope toward Gabby. "That is a severance package. It should give you time to find another position. We'd appreciate it if you'd clear out your work area before leaving today."

"Fired?" The word felt foreign in her mouth. She'd been with the paper since her sophomore year in college, working her way from intern to section editor over the past four and a half years. The copy editor job was next...or so she thought. "I thought I'd been a great asset to the paper."

The woman sighed. "We feel it's best to have fresh blood going into the new year. I know, it's Thanksgiving and Christmas is just around the corner, but I'm sure you understand that this works best for everyone."

Best for everyone? Gabby didn't know how to respond. What could she say? She was so shell-shocked that she could barely think.

Wesley opened the door, indicating they were done.

"If you'll go ahead and see yourself out, we have another appointment scheduled." The woman pointed to the door.

Speechless, Gabby stood and absentmindedly walked to her office. She'd gone from excited about her future with the paper to numb in the span of minutes. Just like that, and her career with the paper was over. She wasn't even sure how to process the whole thing.

The cell phone she'd tucked in her dress pocket rang, and she fished it out. "Hello?"

"I'm sorry. I know you usually work late," Carrie Anne West's chipper voice filtered through the phone.

The sound of her voice was enough to shake Gabby

out of her daze. It was Tuesday, and she was flying into Amarillo the next day to spend Thanksgiving with her and Carrie Anne's families in Caprock Canyon, Texas.

"It's okay," Gabby replied.

"You sound off. Is everything all right?"

Of course, Carrie Anne would pick up on Gabby being upset. They'd been best friends, or more like sisters, since they were born. It made sense because their moms had been lifelong best friends too, going so far as to live across the street from each other their entire lives. They were all like family and even spent the holidays together.

Normally, Carrie Anne would be the first person Gabby would want to tell about what had happened, but she didn't need to spend the holiday with everyone feeling sorry for her.

Gabby swallowed down her disappointment at being fired and responded, "I'm fine. Just tired after working all day."

Carrie Anne paused a second. "Are you sure?"

"Positive." Gabby put as much sunshine and rainbows into the response as she could muster.

"Okay, I have news. I'm getting married!" Carrie Anne squealed.

Gabby gasped. "Israel passed the bar?" Carrie Anne

and Israel had been sweethearts in high school and all the way through college.

"Israel proposed last night, and I said yes." She paused. "I was going to wait until you got here tomorrow, but I couldn't hold it in. I had to tell you."

"I'm so happy for you." Gabby smiled and went in search of a box to pack her things.

Carrie giggled. "Yeah, the letter came yesterday. I knew he'd taken it, but it was a huge surprise when he asked me. He set up a huge celebration with the whole family. Well, as whole as we could get it. He'd promised to ask me as soon as he passed, and he said he wanted to keep his promise."

"I'm sorry I was working late." If she'd known last night that she was getting fired, she wouldn't have silenced her phone and missed her best friend's engagement.

"It's okay. I understand."

Gabby peeked inside the office two doors down from her. A small box filled with reams of paper sat in the corner. She pulled the paper out, figuring if they didn't want her swiping a box, they shouldn't have fired her. "I'm deliriously happy for you."

"We want to get married New Year's Eve."

New Year's Eve? Gabby stopped at her desk. "That fast? Holy cow. You've always wanted a huge wedding.

You can't—" Gabby stopped short. Yeah, they could because money talked, and they had enough Benjamin Franklins to make up an entire choir. "Well, I guess you can now."

A year ago, the West siblings had won the lottery, and now they were billionaires. The whole thing was still unreal to Gabby, but that was mostly because they didn't act any different. They were good people, sweet and hard-working. If anyone deserved to win that kind of money, they did.

Laughing, Carrie said, "Things have changed quite a bit since then. Wyatt—"

"Nope. Don't want to hear it."

"But I need—"

"No, Carrie Anne. I left Caprock Canyon to get away from him, and I don't want to know anything about him. I know he's your brother, but I can't. The only reason I'm coming to Thanksgiving this year is because you told me he wasn't going to be there." Gabby shook her head as she crammed almost five years' worth of accumulated junk into the box. "We talked about this, remember?"

For a second, Gabby thought Carrie Anne would fight her, but instead, she replied, "Yes, I remember."

The very reason she'd stayed close to Caprock Canyon and pursued her journalism degree at Texas

Tech after graduating high school was the hope that Wyatt would finally notice her.

It was a crush she wished she'd never had. Pining for a man that would never see her as more than his little sister's best friend was stupid. A reality that hit her when Wyatt proposed to Lori Edwards—his on-again, off-again girlfriend he'd met on a rodeo tour. Instead of noticing Gabby, one night while she was home on fall break, their families were eating together and the next thing she knew, Wyatt was getting on one knee.

Her heart had shattered that night five years ago, watching him pull out a ring and ask someone else to marry him. It had been Gabby's wake-up call, a nail in the coffin for her. So, she'd returned to her sophomore year of college and applied for a transfer to the College of Charleston, along with an internship at the Charleston Uptown Gazette. She'd been talking about doing it since she couldn't handle watching Wyatt and Lori together, but after the proposal, she didn't hesitate.

Finding out she was accepted to both the college and internship was her sign that she'd made the right call. That spring, she'd packed up, leaving her heart-break and everything she knew behind.

Her parents and sister had wondered why she had

the sudden urge to get out of Texas, and she'd told them that Charleston had a better program for journalism. They hadn't seemed very convinced but let it be.

"Gabby…" Carrie Anne sighed. "Okay, I won't say anything more. I'm sorry. I know how you feel about him."

"Felt. It's over. Crush, then crushed, and I've moved on." Gabby's meddling radar blared. Carrie Anne had given up way too easily. "You did tell me Wyatt was going to be out of town while I'm there, right?" She didn't want to chance running into him at the Thanksgiving dinner. She'd successfully avoided all chances of seeing him since she'd left home, including all holidays.

"If you're over him, then it shouldn't matter."

"So, Wyatt is going to be home."

Carrie Anne groaned. "As far as I know, he isn't. I'm just saying if you were really over him, Wyatt being here wouldn't be a big deal."

Gabby paused as she picked up a picture of her and Carrie Anne. "I *am* over him." She put the picture in the box. It was no secret Carrie Anne wanted Gabby to be an official member of their family, so to thwart her best friend meddling, she added, "In fact, I'm dating someone."

8

A small gasp answered. "You are? Why didn't you tell me? Who is it?"

"Yep, it just started, and he's a coworker." Wow, a double lie in one sentence. There was no dating, and she was no longer employed. It would take a while for the second part of that thought to sink in.

"What's his name?"

A name? Shoot. She should have thought this through a little better before opening her big fat trap. "Tim Redmane. He's a great guy, but like I said, it's still early."

"Ohhh! I'm so happy for you. If that Tim guy is smart, he'll sweep you off your feet, and before you know it, you'll be married too."

"Don't get ahead of yourself, you hopeless romantic."

Sighing heavily, Carrie Anne said, "Fine. At least I get to see you tomorrow. Are you bringing Tim home?"

"No way. It's too early in the relationship." Even more so for a non-existent one.

"Well, I get to meet him before it's too serious. Maybe I can even convince him to get you to move back home."

Laughing, Gabby rolled her eyes. "Carrie Anne, you are a mess, but I love you."

"I love you too."

"You're picking me up at the airport, right?"

Carrie Anne waited a beat and replied, "Uh…actually, I can't. The wedding planner I wanted just had a cancellation and that's the only time she has available to meet, but you will have a ride, I promise. I can't wait to see you after the appointment."

Gabby was a little disappointed that Carrie Anne wouldn't be there to greet her at the airport, but she understood with the wedding being so soon.

"Late night with popcorn and *A Knight's Tale?*" Gabby smiled.

"It wouldn't be Thanksgiving without that."

"Okay, I'll see you tomorrow."

They said their goodbyes, and Gabby ended the call.

Every time she thought about going home, anxiety would nearly cripple her. She'd stayed away from her home and family—her mom, dad, and sister—because of Wyatt. Always coming up with excuses as to why they should visit her. She'd played it off as being swamped at the paper, and to a degree, she was. As an intern, she'd been given all the crummy grunt work and bad hours, including weekends and every federally observed holiday, plus a few the newspaper made up.

Of course, Gabby's family visited her on occasion, but it wasn't the same. Walking the streets of Charleston didn't have the same effect as Caprock Canyon. Heartache wasn't waiting for her around every corner as it did at home. In Charleston, they were just streets, not memories.

Those years she'd worked as an intern had taught her that if she fought hard enough, she could get through anything. Which meant she'd get through going home. Now that she thought about it, five years was a really long time. How much had things changed? How much had she changed? Well, she'd soon find out.

She finished packing up her office, took the office key off her keyring, and with a sigh, she looked around. This was where she'd done most of her growing up. Where she'd learned how to take criticism, meet demands, and stand on her own two feet. It was where she pushed down homesickness...and shed more than a few tears when things were hard. Now what was she going to do?

Setting her wristlet on top, she picked up the box and walked to the door. Giving it one more glance over, she inwardly said goodbye and flicked the light off. At least this was coming at a time when she was headed back to her hometown. With Wyatt not being there this time, she'd be able to get her legs under her.

She'd lick her wounds and then come back with an updated resume and the determination to start over.

At least Wyatt's absence would give her the chance to face memories without an audience. She was different, the town was different, and she could tackle things now that she couldn't when she'd left. Still, the first step was always the hardest. With a little gumption, she'd get through it.

CHAPTER 2

*S*tanding on the front porch of his brother's ranch house, Wyatt West knocked on the door as he set down his duffle bag full of clothes. While he waited for Bear to answer, he turned and swept his gaze across the endless fields in front of him. Man, things sure had changed since he'd left.

All those years of playing the lottery with his brothers, never expecting anything, had turned into a winning jackpot ticket for an astronomical amount the previous year. It was meant to be a way for him and his brothers, Bear, Josiah, and Hunter, to keep in touch after each of them had moved away from home. An excuse to FaceTime and shoot the breeze while they waited for the numbers to be drawn. The last number had flashed on the screen, and almost over night, they'd become billionaires, along with their baby sister, Carrie Anne, of course. They weren't going to leave her out.

The door swung open, and Wyatt turned, smiling. "Hey, man." It had been a while since he'd seen his oldest brother in person. Touring with the rodeo kept him on the road and away from home.

Bear shook his hand. "Hey, what do you think?"

"I can't even believe this is the same house." Wyatt still struggled to think of himself or his family as billionaires. Mostly because he hadn't touched his share yet.

Bear stepped aside to let him in, and Wyatt's mouth dropped open. "Wow. You've done quite a bit with the place." The home had been nearly falling down the last time he'd seen it a year ago, right after being cleared to ride again after his accident.

Caprock Canyon Ranch had closed ten years ago. Several seasons of bad weather and a horrible drought took their toll on the place, and the owners were left with no choice. At the time, Wyatt was fifteen. He'd been plenty old enough to see the effect of a town's primary source of income drying up. He keenly felt the way the loss affected the town of Caprock Canyon and its people. Each year since, more and more businesses closed up and moved. These days, it was mostly a few families left, a mom-and-pop grocery store carrying a few essential items, and a gas station for tourists who got lost.

It was never a secret that his brother Bear dreamed of owning the sprawling nine-hundred-sixty-acre ranch complete with the farmhouse. Bear had spoken often about what he'd do if he ever got the chance to buy it. The second his share of the money hit his account, he'd contacted a real estate agent. Sixty days later, Wyatt's brother was the proud owner of the ranch two hours northeast of Amarillo.

Bear grinned as his gaze swept the foyer. "Yep, it took the whole year and a lot of work, but it's done. Everyone is spending Thanksgiving through New Year's here this year so we can prepare for the wedding. Nothin' like a good dose of family bonding, right?" He chuckled.

"Well, with a house this size, it sure won't feel crowded during the holiday family get-togethers." Wyatt wasn't sure if he liked that or not. There was something about being jammed into a home too small. What were the holidays without a little forced togetherness?

Bear nodded. "Yeah, well, I wanted this to be a place where we would all fit, especially since it's a thirty-minute drive into town. This way, everyone can plan to stay for the weekend if they want to."

Wyatt had to give him that. It would be nice not having to traipse back and forth between places. "I bet Mom and Dad love it."

They'd tried hard to get their parents to claim the lottery money with them, but their dad wouldn't budge. He wasn't taking money from his children. It was the father's job to provide, not the other way around. Stubborn old mule.

"They do. I just wish they hadn't been so pig-headed about claiming the money with us."

Of course, he and his siblings hadn't let their parent's refusal to take some of the money keep them from paying everything off. Not only had they paid their parents' debt off, but Amos and Pauline Fredericks's too. Family was family, after all, and the Fredericks were like family too. At least, that's what they all thought.

"Is that Wyatt?" his sister called.

Carrie Anne had FaceTimed him the night before to tell him about her exciting news. Wyatt met her at the first-floor stair landing and swooped her into a hug. "I can't believe my baby sister is getting married!"

Carrie Anne laughed as he set her back down. "What can I say, I found my guy."

Israel was a good guy, too, a straight arrow, and there was no doubt he loved Carrie Anne. "Yeah, I guess he's okay. I'm surprised he didn't wait until Thanksgiving dinner and ask you in front of the whole family."

"He got the letter, set the dinner up with Mom and Dad, and asked. I couldn't and wouldn't say no." Her eyes glittered, and it warmed him to see his little sister so happy. At the same time, it put a spotlight on how lonely he was.

With as much as he traveled for the rodeo, it wasn't fair to start something he couldn't finish. Plus, that kind of stress never helped a relationship grow. In town one minute, gone two months in a row. That was no way to figure out if you could start a life with someone. He'd learned that lesson the hard way with his last girlfriend, Lori Edwards.

"Am I the last one home?" asked Wyatt as Bear joined them at the foot of the stairs.

"No," Bear said, shaking his head. "Hunter and Josiah will be here tomorrow."

Carrie Anne turned to Wyatt. "That reminds me. Gabby's flying in tomorrow, and I promised I'd find someone to pick her up. Would you mind doing it?"

"Gabby?" She was his little sister's best friend, like a second sister to him. He hadn't seen her in years. Most of the time when their families were going to visit her, he'd have an event coming up and couldn't go. He didn't mind picking her up and looked forward to seeing her, but he'd just gotten home after being on the road most of the last year.

"Yeah, and I don't want her stranded at the airport on her first visit home in five years. I've asked everyone, and they're all busy. Even Bandit. He's going to Lubbock tomorrow to visit his uncle."

Wyatt liked Gabby, but he was hoping to stay put for a second. "Why can't Bear do it?"

"I can't," Bear interjected. "Dad, Amos, and I are going to take the ATVs out and look over the property. I have a meeting with a cattle broker on Monday, and I need their input on getting this ranch working again now that the house is finished."

"That makes sense." Both of the older men had worked for the ranch when they were in their late teens and early twenties. They'd seen it in its prime. Getting their input on how things should be was a good idea.

"Plus, I told Mom and Dad that I'd be taking care of Thanksgiving dinner this year." Bear grinned.

Wyatt chuckled. "Which means Bandit is doing the actual cooking."

Bear shrugged. "He's my best friend, and he

THE BEST FRIEND'S BILLIONAIRE BROTHER

needed a job. I'm trying to convince him to open his own restaurant, but he'll hear none of it. Told him I'd do a contract and everything, and he's still telling me no."

"He doesn't want your friendship ruined over money." Carrie Anne touched Bear's shoulder. "I think that's sweet."

"Yeah, but what good is money if you can't share it?"

"Do Mom and Dad suspect we're getting their house redone?"

Shaking his head, Bear smiled and said, "Nope, Carrie Anne and I have it all planned."

Carrie Anne nodded as her lips broke into a wide mischievous grin. "They're leaving for Hawaii in February for an entire month. It's perfect because they'll just think we're treating them to an anniversary gift."

"If they'd just taken some of the money, it wouldn't be a big deal." Bear crossed his arms over his chest. "Don't know why Dad has to be so stubborn."

Carrie Anne and Wyatt raised their eyebrows simultaneously, snickering as they did.

"You've got no clue, huh?" Wyatt asked. His brother was as bull-headed as they came.

Bear narrowed his eyes. "Shut up." He trudged off,

19

and the next thing Wyatt heard was the back door slamming shut.

"What gopher crawled up his britches?" Wyatt asked.

Carrie Anne looked in the direction Bear went. "He's still hurting."

"That was a year ago. He needs to move on." He paused. "Not everyone is out for our money."

She leaned back. "And you're one to talk."

Wyatt rolled his eyes. "I'm traveling too much to even think about a relationship. It wouldn't be fair."

"You are a lousy liar. Just admit Lori threw you for a loop."

"She didn't."

Carrie Anne lifted a single eyebrow and pinched her lips together.

"I'm telling you, I'm fine. I just…haven't found the right woman yet." *Right* being the operative word. Sure, there were plenty of women hanging around the rodeo who were willing and ready, but Wyatt wanted more. He wanted family, home, and belonging.

"Back to Gabby, *will* you pick up Gabby for me? You're the only one left to do it." She grumbled under her breath about dealing with fire later.

"Did you say something about fire?" he asked.

She waved him off. "No, just talking to myself. So will you get her?"

"Yeah, I'll pick her up. I haven't seen her in ages."

"Well, when I talked to her this morning, she said she was dating some guy named Tim." Carrie folded her arms over her chest. "But I don't believe her for a second."

Wyatt felt a little kicked. Gabby dating? Then again, she wasn't so little anymore, as evidenced by his sister tying the knot in six weeks. "Why?"

Carrie Anne stared at him a second like she was waiting for him to say something and then sighed. "Men are so dumb." She spun on her heels and bounced up the stairs. "Just so, so dumb." Her voice trailed off as she left Wyatt standing there gawking after her.

What did that even mean? How was he dumb? Shaking his head, he grabbed his bag and followed Carrie Anne. He'd be spending some time at home, hoping that he could figure between now and the next rodeo if he should dive in harder or hang it up. Maybe by the new year, he'd have his answer and a plan in place.

CHAPTER 3

*W*inding her way through Amarillo airport, Gabby wondered who would be picking her up. At least Wyatt wasn't an option. He was at a rodeo two states over. She'd double-checked the night before just to be safe. And Carrie Anne wouldn't do that to her anyway.

With a quick stop at the arrivals counter, she found where her luggage would be coming in and finished her trek through the airport. The same crowd she'd shared her plane with began to gather, waiting for their suitcases too.

Suddenly, she had the feeling she was being watched. She swept her gaze across the sea of people and froze. Wyatt West.

"No," she whispered. It wasn't possible. He was in

23

Arkansas. She'd checked and double-checked. Even that morning when she'd pulled up the event, he was still listed as a bull rider.

Gabby was going to give Carrie Anne the chewing-out of a lifetime when she saw her. How could she send Wyatt?

What was Gabby going to do now? How much would a ride from Amarillo to Caprock Canyon cost? Whatever it was, it would be worth it not to be trapped in a vehicle with him for two hours. Just as she was plotting her way out, their gazes locked.

Hat in hand, he smiled that signature smile of his. The kind where one side of his lips quirked up and just a bit of his teeth showed. She had a list of her favorite smiles, and this one was the humdinger of them all. It was the kind that made her feel light-headed and stupid.

And she was stupid. He was a married man of many years now. She'd even seen the invitation. Not that she was spying, really. She couldn't help that it had shown up on her mom's Facebook timeline as one of the choices Lori was considering.

In the time that it took for him to reach her, she'd somewhat gathered her thoughts. She was the little sister's best friend, and he was married. It wasn't like they really ran in the same circles in high school, even though she was only a year behind.

When he moved in like he was going to hug her, she crossed her arms over her chest and cocked her hip, stopping him in his tracks. "I thought you were going to be out of town."

Wyatt blinked. "Are you mad? I haven't seen you in five years."

For a second, she stared at him, and then she let her arms fall to her sides. "No. Carrie Anne just said someone was picking me up. I didn't question her because the last time we spoke, she said you had a rodeo event during Thanksgiving weekend and you wouldn't be home." No way was she going to confess she'd double-checked it.

He scratched the back of his neck with his free hand. "Well, I was supposed to be at an event, but it got canceled due to weather."

"That's—" She caught herself before finishing the sentence. Why hadn't that been on the events website page? "Oh."

Wyatt held her gaze with his eyebrows knitted together. "Are you upset that I'm picking you up?"

Yes, but he didn't need to know that, and now she was stuck with him because finding another way home would lead to questions she didn't want to answer. "No, I'm fine." Then she noticed a jagged line along his jaw and stepped closer. "Is that a scar along your jaw?"

Stepping in to get a better look was a mistake. Whatever cologne or aftershave he wore swirled around her, and the scent made her skin tingle. A rush of memories and longing hit her so hard her heart physically hurt.

"Yeah, I got bucked bad a couple of years back. Broke a few bones and got this scar and a couple more you can't see. I couldn't afford plastic surgery at the time, and to be honest, I like them because it reminds me to remain humble."

Carrie Anne had mentioned he'd been in a bad accident. She'd even seen a few pictures, but in person, it hit her a little harder. "Carrie Anne said you'd been in an accident. I'm sorry you were hurt."

He nodded. "I was lucky it wasn't worse." Pausing, his gaze roamed over her face. "You sure look different."

The words sobered her. Stepping back, she held his gaze. "I am different."

"I guess we all are, huh?"

"Maybe." Her gaze traveled to his hand. Where was his wedding band? He'd never struck Gabby as a man who would get married and then run around pretending he wasn't. "Is Lori okay with you not wearing your wedding band?"

"Lori? I'm not married."

"What?" she asked softly.

Wyatt's eyebrows drew together. "Didn't Carrie Anne tell you? I would have thought she'd have wasted no time telling you. I never married Lori. She…never mind." He paused and cast his gaze to the floor. "It's been over with her for a while now."

Over? For a while? But the invitations. "I just figured…by now—" She stopped short.

A little sprig of hope hit so hard, she felt gut-punched. But she got ahold of it quick. Wyatt was never going to be interested in her, and the feeling was mutual. She'd repeat that until it stuck.

"She wasn't good enough for you anyway." The sentence slipped out before she could stop it.

He lifted his head and narrowed his eyes. "Why would you say that?"

She waved him off. It didn't matter now, did it? Gabby was over him, and he was probably dating someone else. "It's water under the bridge. I need to get my luggage. Mom and Dad are expecting me to be there when they get home."

"My understanding is that we're all staying at Casa Bear through the holidays."

She blinked a few times as she tried to process what Wyatt had said. She would only be there for Thanksgiving weekend, not all the holidays, but staying with the Wests for even five days? As in, in the same vicinity as Wyatt? Clearly, the start of the holidays had been declared open season on Gabby Fredericks. Was this another thing Carrie Anne didn't tell her? "What?"

"Bear invited our families to spend the weekend at the ranch house for Thanksgiving. It's all fixed up and ready to go. He did a bang-up job on it too. Looks like a brand-new house in my opinion."

"Oh." She nodded as her gaze traveled to the floor, muttering to herself, "The weekend. I can do that."

"I'm sorry. I didn't catch that last part," Wyatt said.

Yeah, and she wasn't providing a net. She smiled as she brought her gaze back to his. "Nothing. This'll be great. I won't have to divide my time between my family and Carrie Anne." She turned and walked to the nearly empty conveyor belt.

Wyatt kept pace with her, stopping at the same time she did. Awkward silence fell between them as they waited for her luggage. Her large red bag rounded the corner, and they both reached for it at the same time.

Their hands touched, and for a second, she thought

she'd actually been hit with electricity. Then the lingering jolt rolled like a wave from her hand, up her arm, and settled in the pit of her stomach, setting her heart racing. No, no, no, she couldn't let that happen. She was home to spend time with her family. There'd be no…whatever it was that just happened. She'd wear gloves if necessary.

Gabby jerked her hand back, and he pulled her luggage off the belt. Laughing, she said, "Staticky."

He caught her gaze a second and then nodded. "Yeah, I guess it was."

She turned on her heels, and looking over her shoulder, she said, "The quicker we get on the road, the quicker we get there."

As she reached the door, she nearly tripped over herself getting out of the airport. The brisk wind took her breath away and gave her goosebumps. "Holy cow, it's cold." It got cold in Charleston, but the wind there was nothing like the winds in the Panhandle. This air felt like it had sharp claws and fangs.

"Oh, it's even colder now," Wyatt said as he joined her outside, setting his hat on his head.

"I should have watched the weather closer. It wasn't nearly this cold in Charleston." Not even close. She hadn't remembered it ever being this cold. Had she thought about it, she'd have brought long underwear.

He set her luggage down and slipped out of his coat. "Here, that little blouse of yours is no match for West Texas winds." He smiled and helped her put it on.

"Yeah." Except she wasn't thinking west wind lowercase, she was thinking West wind. With one tiny whiff, his scent washed over her, and she was a teenager again, endlessly scribbling Mrs. West on the edges of her school notebooks. Little hearts and plus signs.

The longer she was around him, the clearer it became that she wasn't prepared to deal with him just yet. How was she going to make it through the holiday while spending the night in the same house as him?

Another sharp gust blew, and Wyatt grabbed her luggage. "Actually, you stay here and get back inside. I'll go get the truck. Don't want that pretty face of yours getting chapped from all this harsh wind."

Before she could gather her wits or her words, Wyatt was out of earshot. He'd said pretty face. He'd only done that once before, on the night of her senior prom. He and Bear had been outside, playing football, and she'd walked across the street to meet up with Carrie Anne.

Just as her foot had hit the sidewalk, Wyatt had

looked her way and said, "Whoa," right before taking a hit to the stomach. She'd run over to him, and just as he looked up, he'd called her beautiful.

That single word had taken her crush to a whole new level. She'd gone from being slightly infatuated to full-blown out of her mind for him. To her reasoning, a guy didn't call a girl beautiful for no reason. From that moment on, Wyatt had held her heart...until he proposed to Lori. A woman he hadn't even married.

Why hadn't he married Lori, anyway? Gabby never thought Lori was the right girl for him, but Wyatt was over the moon for her. She was a little on the stuck-up side and a lot self-absorbed. More than once, she'd broken up with him just so she could date another guy for a week or two, only to come around again. They were always breaking up and getting back together. She never understood it. Which was another reason why Gabby had been so shocked when he asked Lori to marry him. How could he marry a girl who seemed to only love him when it was convenient? Maybe it hadn't made sense to him either and that's why he didn't marry her.

NO! her head screamed, drowning out anything her heart might have to say. No. Not this time. She wasn't a little girl with a crush anymore. She was a grown woman in charge of her life, emotions, and actions. There was no way she was going to allow herself to get hung up on him again. It would lead nowhere except heartache, and she'd had enough of that to last her a lifetime. This time it would be different. She'd be different.

THIRTY MINUTES INTO THE DRIVE, the awkward silence in Wyatt's truck was enough to smother Gabby. He was an arm's length away and looking better than she'd ever seen him. Those blue eyes of his made her insides blaze every time he threw a look in her direction. Even the way he held the steering wheel was making her batty. Something had to give, or she'd never make it to Caprock Canyon with her sanity.

"So, you still love the rodeo?" she asked. If she was going to be stuck with him, she may as well try to find ways to dislike him. He'd always been a little cocky when it came to the rodeo, and she had a whole weekend to get through.

Glancing at her, he laughed. "Well, aside from the broken bones, I've loved it. The travel, the crowds, the whole shebang has been fun. It's been an experience."

The response wasn't what she expected, and the broken bones still surprised her. The love for it, well, he'd loved bull riding since she could remember. As soon as he turned eighteen, he'd turned pro. She could see the twinkle in his eyes anytime he talked about it. When he first started riding bulls, the whole family would go watch him. He'd finish his eight seconds, land on his feet like a superhero, and his face would light up with a smile so spectacular it made her almost swoon.

"How about you? Have you liked living in Charleston?" he asked.

Loaded question. Before she got fired, she would have been looking forward to returning to Charleston. She'd loved working for the paper, and she'd worked hard to climb the ladder, moving from intern to full-time employee right after she graduated from college. Anytime they needed someone for a story, no matter how demeaning it may have seemed, she'd eagerly volunteered.

Her coworkers had been great, but she'd never made an effort to be more than work friends. Sure, they'd go out on an occasional night and have some dinner and maybe some wine and talk about the paper or where they saw print newspaper going. Come to think of it, none of their conversations ever got beyond work. The magnifying glass she suddenly had wasn't making her feel all that anxious to go back.

"Uh, yeah, it's so pretty." And it was. Gabby loved Battery Park. "All the trees, the ocean, the historical places. I spent my first year just visiting different places. It's really nice, and the people are friendly."

"Carrie Anne says you're dating a guy named Tim."

Carrie Anne told Wyatt that? Oh, that rotten girl. She was definitely up to something. More than likely, she was calling Gabby's bluff, but Gabby would show Carrie Anne. Her relationship with Tim just got a whole lot more real. "Yep, been seeing him a couple of weeks."

"Any potential there?"

It took effort not to laugh hysterically, but some-how, she managed to hold it back. Instead, she shrugged. "I don't know. It's too soon to really tell. I mean, it takes longer than a couple of weeks to get to know someone." That was a reasonable response. One that could be easily sold. "How about you? Are you dating anyone?"

He shook his head as he returned his gaze to the road ahead. "No. Traveling makes it hard to really get to know someone. It also shows you if a relationship can handle rough times."

Is that what happened with him and Lori? Why didn't Lori just go with him? "Is it too much prying to ask what happened with you and Lori?"

His lips pressed together, and a second later, he said, "We just weren't meant to be." It was a tone she'd heard before. One that meant the conversation was over.

Instead of pressing him like she wanted to, Gabby turned her focus to the scenery flashing past. If he didn't want to talk about it, there wasn't much she could do, and she didn't care anyway. It wasn't like when they were younger when he'd sometimes come find her when he couldn't find Carrie Anne, asking about girls and relationships. More than once, they'd talked about deep things like marriage and family. But now they were older and had grown apart.

Silly youthful notions, but those little talks were what started her crush. She liked that he wanted to find someone, settle down, and get married. He wanted a small house and a big yard so his family would spend time outside. He wanted Friday nights with no cell phones and local football games.

He'd wanted all the same things she wanted. A simple life with the love of her life and kids running around. Small-town life.

But he'd always wanted those things with someone else. And that little piece of knowledge was what she needed to remember this weekend, especially if she was to keep her feet on the ground.

On occasion, one of them would break the silence by pointing out animals or something interesting. Other than that, it was just a long stretch of highway until they got closer to Caprock Canyon.

Gabby could feel the change in elevation. The way the air seemed to grow cooler. This part of the Panhandle felt like its own little world. It was hotter in the summer and colder in the winter. It snowed more in Caprock Canyon than just about anywhere around.

It wasn't until Wyatt was turning off the main road that it hit her. "I can't believe Bear did it. He actually bought the place."

Laughing, Wyatt nodded. "Well, I believe it, but, yeah, I know what you mean. None of us ever expected to win all that money."

She turned to him. "Have you done anything with it?" There literally was no telling with Wyatt. Of the four brothers, he was the most spontaneous.

"I haven't touched a single cent. We had the money deposited in one account initially. You know, so we could all pitch in to pay off family stuff. Once we had that done, then we split it. I didn't want the excitement of winning to cloud my judgment and for me to do something stupid with it, so there it still sits."

Gabby narrowed her eyes. She knew by the way he said it that he was holding something back. "And?"

"And what?"

"What else?"

"What makes you think there's something else?" He shot her a glare.

She cocked an eyebrow. "I've known you all my life. I just know."

"Can we just drop it?" His lips curled as he said it. "I hate talking about it."

Gabby leaned back, moving as close to the door as she could. He'd never snapped at her like that. Never. "Okay," she whispered.

A wall of uncomfortable silence fell between them, and the few miles from the road to the ranch house felt like forever.

As soon as the truck pulled to a stop, Wyatt turned to her. "Gabby, I'm—"

She threw the door open and jumped out. "I guess my time away hasn't changed things as much as I thought." She slammed the door then yanked open the back door and grabbed her luggage, ignoring the biting cold that hit her face.

Wyatt got out of the truck and came around the bed. "Really, Gabby, I'm sorry."

"Just..." What was there to say? He needed to leave her alone. Seeing him brought back so many feelings and emotions, and as much as she wanted to deny it, there was still that *something* Wyatt had that was pulling her to him.

He reached for her luggage, but she jerked it away. "I've been on my own and alone long enough. I don't need help." She pulled on the handle of the suitcase, the wheels digging into the dirt. "Why can't he just... leave me alone," she whispered to herself.

Why did he have to be in town in the first place? And why couldn't the torch she had for him ever die? What was wrong with her? She'd never considered herself a glutton for punishment. The second she saw him in the airport, she should have marched her happy self to the ticket counter and gone back to Charleston.

Now she was stuck with a man she couldn't have... and, by golly, didn't want. Maybe if she repeated that phrase enough times, she wouldn't actually want him anymore.

CHAPTER 4

*W*yatt swore under his breath and kicked one of the tires on the truck. When he'd agreed to pick up Gabby, he hadn't expected to pick up a beautiful woman. The last image he had of her from before she'd left for South Carolina was of a fresh-faced college sophomore, but now she was replaced by the gorgeous woman who'd just stomped into the house. The only thing seemingly unchanged was her favorite color, red.

Wow. The little girl he'd always considered a sister wasn't giving him brotherly feelings at all. When she'd stepped close to him to look at his scar, he'd just taken a deep breath. It had been the worst—or best—timing. He couldn't quite decide. Gabby's perfume had smelled incredible. And her lips? When did they get so…luscious? Dang, when did she get so beautiful?

He quickly followed Gabby into the house and paused a second, watching her fight to get up the stairs with her luggage. Man, oh, man, Gabby definitely wasn't a little kid anymore. The deep red blouse paired with dark wash jeans showed off her figure. Her long dark hair fell past her shoulders and curled up at the ends.

He took a deep breath, shaking away the strange reaction. Yanking off his hat, he sighed and hung it on a hook by the door. He crossed the foyer and reached for the handle. "Let me help you with that."

She popped his hand. "I can get it."

"Clearly, you can't, or you would have already. It's heavy. Just admit you need help."

"No. Not from you." She stopped and glared at him. "Leave me alone."

"I said I was sorry, and I meant it. I'm…what do I need to say to make you believe me?" She had seemed angry with him since the moment she saw him at the airport, and he had only made it worse. Why had she cared that he had picked her up and that he was there and not at the rodeo?

Gabby looked away. "You've never snapped at me like that."

"I know, and I shouldn't have. You were asking an innocent question, and I bit your head off. It's not you; it's me. I'm…" He set his hands on his hips and swore under his breath. "I'm…lost lately. I am sorry, Gabby. You're one of my oldest friends, and I never should have spoken to you like that."

"Friend," he thought he heard her mutter. She grumbled something else he couldn't make out and began fighting with her luggage again.

He pushed her hand aside, took the handle, and began walking up the stairs. "I'm helping whether you want me to or not."

She stomped up after him, her boots clacking on the wood. "Give me my luggage."

"No. I said I was sorry, and now I'm being a gentleman and helping." He didn't even bother to slow down. When they got to the top of the landing, she tried to take the handle, and he jerked it away. "I've got it."

Her lips pinched together, and her little nose scrunched up. Man, she was cute when she was mad. Had she always been so cute? "I can get it from here."

"Do you know what room you're staying in?" Bear had told Wyatt that morning before he left to get Gabby that her room was the last room on the left. Wyatt had initially taken the first room on the right, but now he was going to move into the room right across from her just so he could bug her.

Squaring her shoulders, she lifted her chin. "No, but I can figure it out. Thank you."

"You have always been so stubborn."

In a split second, she snaked her hand out and pinched his stomach so hard he nearly yelped. "You take that back. I'm not the stubborn one. You are."

Wyatt rubbed his stomach. "Ouch. That wasn't fair."

"No," she said, taking the handle of her luggage and smiling. "But you let go of my luggage."

Oh, that did it. He took her by the waist, threw her over his shoulder, and didn't stop walking until he reached her room. He plopped her on the bed and without a single word went back for her luggage. When he returned, judging by the murderous look she was giving him and the way she was standing with legs apart and hands clenched at her sides, she was going to strangle him.

She crossed the room and pointed her finger at him. "If you ever, and I mean ever, do that to me again, I will—"

He leaned in, narrowing his eyes, and she stopped short. "You'll what?"

Her eyebrows drew in further. "I don't know, but I'll think of something that will make you regret it."

Even mad as a hornet, she was breathtaking. She'd always been feisty, not taking junk from anyone. Memories played in his mind of when they were younger. It didn't matter how big the other person was, if Gabby saw them picking on someone smaller than them, she'd tear them up. Most of the time, she'd have them running home crying, and she hadn't even hit them.

A smile spread on Wyatt's lips. "I know how you get. You were being difficult, and I had to do something."

She shook her head. "You didn't have to do that."

No, but it worked. He pulled her into a hug. "I'm glad you're home, Gabby. I've missed you."

She pushed against him at first, but he squeezed tighter. Slowly, she thawed and hugged him back. "I've missed you too," she whispered.

The longer the hug continued, the weirder it got. It felt so right to have her in his arms. She fit more perfect than anyone ever had. He leaned back, and his heart jackhammered. More than just fitting perfect, she *was* perfect. Soft bronze skin, dark eyes, and round cheeks. And was that honeysuckle perfume she was wearing? Whatever it was only enhanced her essence, making his nerves tingle.

What was he doing? The nails ran down the chalkboard so slow and loud in his mind that he nearly covered his ears. He dropped his arms and stepped back. "Uh, well, I, uh, I'm sorry for earlier."

"I know." Her rosy lips stretched into a soft smile. "What room are you staying in?"

His head said, *First room on the right*, but his wires crossed the message, and he replied, "Across the hall." He blinked. That wasn't true. Why did he say that? They'd made up now, and he didn't need to get back at her. "I mean—" But he wanted to be across the hall. It meant he'd open his door and possibly see her each day she was home. He liked that idea even more than coming clean.

"Mean what?"

"Oh, just that I guess I need to let you get settled."

"Okay." A puzzled look crossed her features. "Where is everyone?"

"Well, our moms went with Carrie Anne to meet the wedding planner. You *know* our moms are going to be involved. Bear is out riding around on one of the ATVs with our dads. He wants their opinion on how to get things going. And I don't know where Josiah or Hunter are. Have you talked to your sister?"

Gabby shook her head. "Not since yesterday, and you know Stephanie. She's about like you when it comes to spontaneity."

He laughed. "Yeah, I guess we both get wild hairs."

"Do you know when any of them will get back?"

"No, but I'm hungry. I'm sure Bandit could cook us something, or we could even run into town for a bite. I mean, if you're hungry or—" He stopped short, wondering why he was suddenly a babbling idiot. He didn't get flustered around women, so what was his problem?

She looked over her shoulder at the bed. "I think I might take a nap."

"That doesn't sound half bad."

A wide smile lifted her cheeks, and her eyes twinkled. "You remember when we were kids and we'd camp out? We'd all pile into the same tent 'cause we were afraid of the coyotes. We were such wimps."

"Yeah, I seemed to always manage to have my sleeping bag next to yours."

"I'd hold your hand. You'd scoot in close and tell me you'd protect me." She cleared her throat. "Well, me and Carrie Anne, because she'd be right there with me."

Wyatt nodded. "Yeah, coyotes were the only thing

you were afraid of, but instead of running inside, you'd stick it out. Unlike Carrie Anne."

She looked down and giggled. "Because I didn't want anyone to think I was a chicken."

He tipped her chin up with one finger. "You were never a chicken."

Their eyes locked, and he found himself lost in the depths of hers. So deep and dark and full of mysteries he wanted to solve.

"*Hey!*" Carrie Anne squealed as she bounded into the room.

Wyatt jumped back and swallowed hard. What had just happened? If he didn't know any better, another minute or two, and he'd have kissed Gabby. And she was dating someone. He needed some air to clear his head.

Gabby grabbed Carrie Anne, and they swayed back and forth as they hugged.

"Uh, I guess I'll let you two catch up," Wyatt said, his voice husky.

"Oh, Wyatt." Gabby slipped off his coat, and their fingers brushed as she handed it to him, causing his pulse to jump. "Thanks," she said with a sweet smile.

He swallowed. "Uh, sure."

Stepping back, he nearly tripped over himself to get out of her room. He'd known Gabby forever. Their families were sewn together like blood, only stronger. It wasn't right to think of her like something other than a friend...a little sister. Whatever was getting his wires crossed needed to stop.

Slowly, he shook his head. She was also dating a guy named Tim. If there was one thing Wyatt wasn't, it was a cheater...and he didn't help women cheat either.

Why was he even thinking that? It was complete nonsense. The only thing he could figure was that he was lonely. It might not be the best time for a relationship, but he sure did want one. And not a little fling. He wanted the next relationship to go somewhere with someone he could see growing old with. That was all this shock surrounding Gabby was—a little kick in the pants to wise up and put himself out there again.

As he slipped inside his room, he stared at the duffle bag sitting on top of the bed.

What was he going to do? He'd told her he was staying across the hall. If he didn't, either she'd think he'd lied or he was avoiding her. He wasn't between a rock and a hard place. He was in a rockslide.

Eh, he'd still change rooms. There was a chance she'd be stubborn again.

He laughed at himself. Man, he'd spent too much

time on the road and not enough time at home. His reaction was due to loneliness. Nothing else. With a little time, everyone would find their rhythm again, and everything would be back to normal.

CHAPTER 5

Carrie Anne squeezed Gabby a little harder. "Oh, how I've missed you. I'm so glad you're home."

Gabby returned the almost too-tight hug. "It's good to be home. I've missed you too. All of you."

Her friend leaned back. "Wyatt especially, huh?"

Pulling away, Gabby walked to her bed and sat on the edge. "I can't let myself think that way, Carrie Anne. He doesn't see me like that. It's never going to happen. And I told you, I'm dating someone."

"And that's hogwash. You can't sell that to me."

Narrowing her eyes, Gabby crossed her arms over her chest. She should have known Carrie Anne would meddle. "Fine. I made him up because I didn't want you pressuring me. Is that why you set me up?"

"I didn't set you up. Everyone else was busy. Wyatt was the only one who was available."

"Pretty stinkin' convenient. The one man I don't want to see, and I have to spend two hours with him and nowhere else to go."

Then add being tossed over his shoulder like a flour sack and carried to her room. And that weird hug that lasted almost too long. For a second, it even looked like he might kiss her. Already, her mind was playing tricks on her, and it'd only been a couple hours.

Carrie Anne joined Gabby on the bed. "Well, regardless, I know you and Wyatt would be great together if you guys would give it a chance."

"If you love me at all, you'll stop. I'm begging you to stop. I'm here through Thanksgiving weekend, and I just want to relax."

Before Carrie Anne could respond, a light tapping came from the door. "Can I come in?" Gabby's mom, Pauline, asked.

Gabby jumped up and met her mom halfway, giving her a hug. "Hey, Mom."

"Where's my hug?" Carrie Anne's mom, Caroline, asked with waiting open arms. Gabby hugged her too. "Oh, it's so good to see you." Mrs. West held her out. "Oh my word, I think you've gotten even prettier."

Waving her off, Gabby shook her head. "You always say that."

"Because it's true." She smiled.

Gabby's sister, Stephanie, laughed as she hugged Gabby. "Hey, it's good to see you!"

Gabby returned the hug and said, "You too."

Stephanie dropped her arms and stepped back. "This house is amazing, am I right?"

Nodding, Gabby smiled. "Bear did an incredible job, but I'm not surprised. He's only talked about this ranch since he could speak."

"True. Still, it's wow-inducing. Big enough for our families, but not so big you get lost. I love how homey it feels. I especially love the peace and quiet." Her sister turned her attention back to Gabby.

Peace and quiet? Gabby could use some of that. "Yeah, out in the middle of nowhere, I think you should expect that." She laughed.

Mrs. West looked at her daughter. "Carrie Anne, did you ask her yet?"

Gabby looked from Mrs. West to Carrie Anne. "Ask me what?"

Carrie Anne stood and chewed her bottom lip. "I wanted to see if there's a chance you can stay until the wedding. I have dress fittings, food tasting, all the things that go with a wedding, and I can't imagine doing those things without you. I know it's last minute, but you've hardly taken any time off from work. Do you think they'd be okay with you staying until New Years?"

Six weeks? In Caprock Canyon? With Wyatt? Her heart wilted. The thought of five days had been bad enough. But this was Carrie Anne. Her best friend in the whole wide world. She could be a pest, know-it-all, instigator, and every other annoying thing possible, but Gabby loved her. If the roles were reversed, there was no way Gabby could get married without Carrie Anne by her side.

It wasn't like she had a job anyway. Not that she'd spill that just yet. Plus, there was no one waiting for her in Charleston either. It would just be her, looking for jobs and nothing else to do.

"I'd have to call the paper and ask, but I don't think they'd mind." Gabby didn't like the fib, but the last thing she wanted right now was to talk about her job situation. Not only would Carrie Anne try to fix it, but she'd be begging Gabby to move back home. Something she couldn't do just yet.

Carrie Anne clapped her hands, jumped up and down, and then grabbed Gabby in a bear hug. "I'm so glad you can stay."

Laughing, Gabby hugged her. "I didn't say I could. I said I'd call and ask. They may very well want me back."

"Do I need to bribe them?" Carrie leaned back as she asked.

"No."

Gabby's mom smiled. "I certainly would love for you to stay for a while. It's been a long time since you've been home."

"Me too. It's been a long time since I've had the chance to really hang out with my little sister," Stephanie added.

Pulling free from Carrie Anne, Gabby looked at her mom and sister. "You've visited me in Charleston."

"It's not the same thing, honey," her mom replied.

Mrs. West nodded. "Absolutely not the same. Having your babies home gives mommas peace of mind. It doesn't matter how old you are; we worry."

Carrie Anne rolled her eyes. "Mom, you're so dramatic."

"I am not." She chuckled. "Anyway, everyone is waiting on us to start eating."

Hooking her arm in Gabby's, Carrie Anne grinned. "This is going to be awesome. We can talk colors after dinner. I told the wedding planner we'd have a decision by tomorrow. She said we'll need to make them quickly if we plan to pull this wedding off by New Year's Eve."

They followed their moms out of the room, still linked together and Carrie Anne talking a mile a minute. Once they reached the formal dining room, Gabby looked around in awe. It was open and bright and warm.

Whoever Bear had hired had done an incredible job here. The walls were painted warm hues of blue-gray, with pictures hung that complimented the rustic farmhouse table running the middle of the room. It wasn't some cavernous space, but it did have more room than their families' homes in Caprock Canyon.

Based on the plates of meat, cheeses, and various condiments, they were doing sandwiches. It made sense because they'd be eating such a heavy Thanksgiving meal the next day, and she suspected that Bandit was already getting ready for the feast.

The moment everyone realized she'd arrived, it was a hug-fest. Gabby loved it. It had been so long since they'd all been in one room together, and she'd missed how warm it made her feel.

As much as she loved being in Charleston, she loved being home even more. Five years away, and she'd forgotten how much she treasured her little hometown. Being in Caprock Canyon, surrounded by the people she loved, weakened her resolve to return to Charleston.

She glanced around the room and found Wyatt leaning against the far wall, talking to his dad, King. His face was lit up, and even from where she stood, she could see the twinkle in his eyes. Whatever they were discussing had him excited.

That was one of the things she'd loved about him. The way he'd pour all of himself into something. It was always all or nothing with him. The moment he made his choice, he was whole-hog into it. Same as her. Another trait they shared. Not that they spent time talking a lot about it. It was just something she'd noticed.

Wyatt must have sensed her staring and pulled his attention from his dad to her. He shot her a half-smile and straightened, and the next thing Gabby knew, he was weaving through people, walking toward her.

"I'm not wrong," whispered Carrie Anne.

"Hush. You are too," Gabby whispered back.

Wyatt stopped in front of her, a huge grin on his face. "Hey, no nap?"

Chuckling, Gabby shook her head. "Like she'd let me." She tipped her head in Carrie Anne's direction.

"True." He stepped closer. "You gonna sit by me?"

Sit by him? "After you tossed me over your shoulder?" She crossed her arms over her chest. "No."

His mouth dropped open, and his posture wilted. "I said I was sorry."

Gabby shook her head, hiding her smile as she looked away. "I was thinking I'd sit between my mom and Carrie Anne. I suspect she has wedding stuff to tell me about." She shrugged one shoulder, nonchalant.

His lips turned down. "Oh."

"Oh, no. Wedding details are for later. I'm sitting with Israel and Daddy. You're free to sit with Wyatt if you want to, Gabby." Carrie Anne grinned a smidge too brightly.

Gabby pinched her lips together, wishing she could push pause and scream so loud it hurt. What could she do, though? Tell Wyatt she couldn't sit by him? He'd ask why, and Gabby had no good reason. Well, other than her feelings for him, and she was certainly not divulging that information. "Then I guess I'm free."

His smile returned, wider than ever. "Great. I'm sitting at the end." He placed the palm of his hand on the small of her back, making her nearly jump as the tingles spread from his fingertips to the rest of her body. "I think it's quieter down on the end. We can talk and catch up."

The whole world was out to get her. She didn't want to catch up with Wyatt. She didn't want to be sitting next to him looking all gorgeous and smelling so good that it took effort not to lean in and take a big whiff.

They walked together to the end of the table, and he pulled out her chair for her, placing her at the very end of the row, on his right. At the end of the table was her dad, and she hugged him again before taking her seat across from her mom.

Wyatt took his seat next to her and leaned over. "Told you it was a little quieter down here."

His breath tickled her ear, and she giggled.

"What's so funny?" her sister asked. Stephanie had taken a seat next to their mom, with Josiah on her right.

Gabby wrinkled her nose and shook her head. "Nothing, really. Just funny that we're finally all together at a table and it's not suffocating."

Their dad chuckled. "This was really nice of Bear to think of the family like this. He's done a jam-up good job."

Wyatt cleared his throat. "You scouted the property with Bear and Dad, didn't you?"

"I did." Amos paused as he took a drink of water.

"We found a pecan orchard about five miles from here. It's in rough shape, but I think we can save it. It'll need better irrigation. That's if Bear wants to keep it."

Wyatt's mouth dropped open. "A pecan orchard?"

Her dad nodded. "That's what we all thought. I had no idea the Canyons had any such ideas. They must have started it right before they fell on hard times. There's even a rundown old house over there, like they planned on having someone stay there and tend it."

Gabby's gaze drifted to the table as she lost herself in a memory. The summer after his graduation from high school, Wyatt had his tonsils out. She was supposed to go to camp, but Mrs. West was still working at the time. Gabby overheard her fretting about staying home with Wyatt.

In a split-second decision, she offered to stay with him, and then she'd torn up her registration for camp. She'd told Wyatt that her parents had planned a vacation, and then it had fallen through. Of Course, Carrie Anne had picked up on what she was doing the second Gabby said she wasn't going.

Oh, he'd been miserable that week, but Mrs. West had supplied them with enough popsicles to build an igloo. In Gabby's mind, it was a good trade. Not only did she get to spend time with Wyatt, but she got junk food too. Plus, she loved Mrs. West as much as she loved her own family. The look of relief when she'd volunteered was worth just as much as spending time with Wyatt.

She couldn't remember how it had started, but they'd spent the entire week talking about owning an orchard. She was going to bake pies. They were going to have apple-picking days where families would come to the orchard. Once a month, they were going to have a farmer's market so people could buy fresh produce.

Wyatt nudged her with his shoulder, pulling her from her thoughts. "You remember talking about having an orchard? That summer I had my tonsils out? Maybe this could be it."

"Vaguely," she lied.

"When did you two talk about all that?" Gabby's mom asked.

"Oh, quite a few times," Wyatt answered. "I'd go to her with girl trouble from time to time, and we'd wind up talking about all sorts of stuff."

Stephanie tilted her head. "I didn't know that."

Shrugging, Wyatt looked at Gabby. "Well, we had this little spot at the playground by the school. We'd go there when we had stuff on our minds. Sometimes, I'd find her; other times, she'd find me."

Gabby nodded, the memories filling her thoughts with so many good times. She'd loved those moments, especially when they'd grown older. She could remember it like it was just a second ago. They only brought her heartache now.

He smiled. "That summer after my surgery was a rough one. My first time back on a bull was rough. It left me feeling like I had no business being there."

Yep, she remembered that too. He'd looked so hurt and dejected. "You were pretty upset."

He shifted to tap her shoulder with his again. "You told me to put my chin up and keep going. That those seasoned guys might have had a better ride, but they didn't have my style or my drive."

"They didn't," she said and lifted her gaze to his. "You'd finish your eight seconds, hit that ground, and your joy would be infectious. You loved it, and I loved watching you." Her cheeks burned when she realized she'd said all of that out loud. She pulled her gaze from his and avoided any eye contact with her mom or sister. "I mean, everyone loved watching you. That's why we'd all go to your events."

Why had she said all that? Now she was going to look like an idiot. She should have fought harder to sit by Carrie Anne. When was she ever going to learn that being in Wyatt's gravity was only going to make her crash to the ground?

Her heart whispered, *Never*.

Six weeks. She was going to go down in flames.

CHAPTER 6

*G*abby's sister laughed. "Well, not the whole family. She bribed me to drive her to your rodeo events." Stephanie smiled, shaking her head. "One of them even got me a six-month reprieve from trash duty. It was right after you graduated from high school. You'd just joined the Professional Rodeo Cowboys Association, and I think you were somewhere in Oklahoma. The only way mom would let her go was if I drove her. I don't think she ever missed one until she moved to Charleston."

Wyatt's eyebrows knitted together as he thought back to that first year. Even his family hadn't come to *all* his events. A couple of them were upwards of eight hours away, and he didn't remember Gabby being at all of them.

Mrs. Fredericks smiled. "I remember that. He was in…" she paused, tapping her mouth with her finger. "Oh, yeah, Fort Smith, Arkansas, not Oklahoma. There was no way I was letting you drive that far by yourself. I'd taken you to a couple of the ones in and around Dallas and Abilene, but that was just too much distance for my peace of mind."

"You were at the event in Fort Smith?" asked Wyatt.

Nodding, Gabby fidgeted with the napkin next to her plate. "Um, well, your mom had a really bad cold, and your dad didn't want to leave her. That meant no one was going to be there. It was the first time you were in another state. I—"

"But you were there? I never saw you."

Stephanie scoffed. "I know. She made me leave before you could. To this day, I have no idea why she was in such a hurry to leave. We'd driven all that way, and she wouldn't even say hello. It made no sense to me."

Gabby's face was now as bright red as her blouse. "I think we've reminisced enough at this point. Um, so, Dad, you said that there's a pecan orchard. What did Bear think of that?"

Whatever they were talking about, it was white noise to Wyatt. Gabby had shown up for every event.

Why had she done that? They *were* family, and the two of them were pretty close as kids. She was his little sister's best friend and basically a sister. Still, as much as Gabby hated taking out the trash, to trade for that chore for six months? He had no idea what to think.

"All right, everyone, let's settle down." Wyatt's dad's voice boomed over everyone in the room. He'd taken his place at the other end of the table.

Bandit set the last tray of bread down and turned to walk out.

"Where do you think you're going?" his father asked.

"W-w-well, sir, I thought I'd l-l-let your families have your meal in peace."

Mr. West point to the chair next to Bear. "You may have put this meal together, but that doesn't make you any less family. Park it, boy."

Bear laughed. "I told you they'd have you eat with us."

Bandit grumbled, "Sh-sh-shut up, Bear."

Talk about a friendship. Bear and Bandit had been friends since Bandit moved to Caprock Canyon as a teenager. He stuttered a little, and that was all the ammo stupid teenagers needed to pick on someone. Cue Bear West. Of the things Wyatt's brother hated—

well, they all hated—was people being bullies. That type of behavior didn't fly in their family.

Bear was captain of the football team, and he caught rumor of one of his linebackers messing with Bandit. Bear wore that guy out. That day, he brought Bandit home to eat dinner with them. From that point on, they were as thick as thieves. No one dared pick on Bandit ever again.

The guy sure could cook, too. Before his mom passed, she'd opened up a restaurant, and he'd learned from her. He'd tried to keep it afloat after she was gone, but it was a losing battle once the ranch died.

Wyatt's dad cleared his throat. "Now, back to what I was wanting to say." He looked at Bear. "We're all proud of you and the work you've done here. This home is beautiful, and we all want to thank you for letting us invade."

Waving him off, Bear shook his head. "Stop, Dad."

Mrs. Fredericks added, "No, sweetheart. Your dad's right. You did wonderfully. And we all get to stay together, which means your momma and I can sneak coffee together tomorrow morning." She laughed.

Wyatt's mom joined in with a chuckle. "If there's coffee, I'm there." She grinned.

"And, Bandit," his dad continued. "Thank you for staying with us and cooking dinner tomorrow. I want you to know we appreciate you, and I'll have my boys in there peeling potatoes. You just give the word."

Gabby leaned over and whispered, "I've missed this."

Her breath against his ear sent goosebumps down his spine. There was that weird feeling again. "It hasn't been the same without you," he whispered back. Now that he really thought about it, the holidays had been different without her, boring. He'd had no one to talk to. Yeah, he had his siblings, but that wasn't the same.

Talking to Gabby always seemed to give him peace, and he was content when he was with her. The world always had a way of disappearing when they'd go off and talk. Stress would roll off him like raindrops on a tin roof. Things were always better when he was with Gabby.

The conversations soon dialed down to a hum as everyone fixed their sandwiches and ate. Every so often, someone would bring up an old memory from when they were kids, and everyone would get involved in retelling the story. Then the conversation drifted to high school and dating.

He'd dated a few girls in high school, but nothing serious like Carrie Anne. He couldn't remember any of the girls he'd dated wanting to go fishing with him. Only one or two had ever come to his amateur rodeo events. After he went pro, he spent his first year focused on winning national titles so he could apply for the PBR, and it had paid off. After working on his skills, he'd applied and received his membership.

Not too long after that, he'd met Lori. She'd come to some of his events, but he was pretty sure she was just there to flirt with the other guys. At the time, Wyatt hadn't really paid attention because she'd always been a bit of a tease. They were on and off for a year, mostly breaking up because she'd get tired of him being on the road. The last time, she'd made up with him and things were going well, or so he thought. Enough that he'd introduced her to his family and proposed to her in front of all of them. They'd been good a while after that. She seemed to be okay with him being on the road. Then...on a whim, he'd decided to surprise her, only to find her having dinner with another man.

It had broken his heart, but not as much as it should have. That's when he wised up and broke it off. As much as he didn't want to admit it, it had bothered him that she could say she loved him and then go around with another man.

A light elbow to his side brought him out of his thoughts. Gabby's dark eyes were trained on him, and she looked concerned. "You okay?"

"Yeah, I'm fine." He smiled. "This is pretty good, huh?"

For a breath, she held his gaze, and he wondered if she was going to press him. She pulled her gaze from his and fixed it on her plate. "I'm enjoying it." Something in her voice hinted at sadness.

"Are *you* okay?" Wyatt asked.

"Yeah, why?"

"Just the way you said it. You sounded sad."

Shaking her head, she smiled, but he knew her well enough to know it was forced. "I'm not."

That bothered him to a puzzling degree, the kind that wasn't little-sister's-best-friend troubled. He moved closer, whispering, "You'd tell me if you were, right?"

She nodded, but her body language screamed a different answer. Talk about a mystery he needed to solve, but there were too many people around. He needed to get her alone and find out why she was hurting. If it was something he could fix, he would.

How would he get her alone, though? It was cold outside, the house was filled, and there wasn't a nook or cranny that would be safe from listening ears. If it was something deep that she needed kept secret, he wanted her to have the freedom to talk.

After getting a little more than halfway through

her sandwich, Gabby wiped her mouth. "Um, I think I'm going to go to my room for a little while. I need to call work and see if I can get the time off for the wedding planning."

She stood, and Wyatt jumped up. "Uh, yeah, I need to…." He should have thought through the rest of the sentence before opening his mouth. "Unpack." Unpack? Well, he did. Now that he was changing rooms.

"You were here yesterday, weren't you?" Carrie Anne perked up. "Didn't you already unpack?"

Everyone at the table stopped talking and stared at Wyatt. His brain fritzed. Good grief, how could he get out of this mess. "Well, I had, but I decided to change rooms. I don't like that first bedroom, so I'm taking the one across from Gabby. There's too much noise with people coming up the stairs." Whoa. Now he was thinking on his feet.

Carrie Anne's eyes narrowed ever so slightly. "Ohhh-kay."

Gabby tapped his bicep with her elbow. "You told me you were in the room across from me. You mean you weren't?"

"Uh…" Sheesh, he was digging himself a hole so fast that dirt was getting in his eyes. How was he supposed to fix this? "We were arguing, and I was going to pester you for being so stubborn." There. That was the truth.

Gabby rolled her eyes. "Really? What is this, junior high?"

"Sorry." Oh man, what a mess he'd gotten himself into.

Hunter crossed his arms over his chest. "Why would I want to switch rooms with you? I don't want to listen to all that noise either."

If they were alone, Wyatt would thump him. "I'm switching. That's all you need to know." He growled the last few words as a warning to shut up about it.

"Whatever." Hunter rolled his eyes.

Gabby set her silverware on top of her plate and then grabbed it and her glass. Wyatt followed her lead and did the same. They stopped by the kitchen and put their dishes in the sink and were quiet until they reached the top of the stairs.

"I can't believe you planned to switch rooms just to bug me."

He scratched the back of his neck as heat raced to his cheeks. "No, not totally. I'd...wanted to switch rooms."

"Whatever. I guess I'll see you later, then."

She started to walk off, and Wyatt took her hand to

stop her. "You seem sad. Is there anything I can do? I mean, that's what family is for, right?"

Heartbeat after heartbeat pounded, her gaze staying trained on his hand. Slowly, she shook her head and pulled her hand free. "No, I'm fine. I just have some stuff to take care of."

He could hear the tremble in her voice, and she wouldn't meet his gaze. Before he could respond, she briskly walked down the hall and disappeared behind her door. For a second, he was dumbstruck. When his brain caught up, he strode down the hall and knocked on her door. "Gabby?"

Silence.

"Gabby? Are you sure everything is okay?"

"I'm fine, Wyatt," she said, sounding anything but. Was she crying?

Wyatt set his hands on his hips. "If there's something bothering you, you can tell me. I promise I won't tell anyone. Whatever is sitting on your shoulders, you can let me help carry it."

A long sigh. "I appreciate the offer, but I have work to do. I'll talk to you later."

What was going on that she wouldn't talk to him? Well, whatever it might be, she wasn't budging. Maybe over the next couple of days, possibly six weeks if her work let her take off, he could find out what it was that was troubling her.

With one last look, he stepped inside Hunter's room, gathered his brother's things, and took them down to the room Wyatt had occupied the night before. Once he'd thrown his own stuff back in his duffle bag, he strode back to the room across from Gabby.

If nothing else, even if she didn't confide in him, he'd at least get to see her every day, and for some reason, his heart even did a skip. He was losing it.

He shut the door, putting the strange feelings aside. He was just happy Gabby was home. He hadn't seen her in a while, and that's all it was—excitement. The family had missed her. Spending time with her would make it feel like old times, and that's what he was needing most: normal, head-clearing time with his whole family.

CHAPTER 7

"Why are you sneaking around my kitchen?" Bandit asked.

Gabby startled as she stood in front of the fridge and nearly dropped the milk she was holding. "Bandit, by all that's holy, you do that again and I'll let a pack of wild dogs in here."

His rich laughter filled the room, and she hushed him. "You're going to wake everyone up!"

Bandit shrugged. "Aw, th-th-they can't hear m-m-me. What are you t-t-trying to put together anyway?"

"I was thinking hot chocolate."

He crossed the kitchen, stopping as he got to her. "That's n-n-no way to make hot chocolate. You gotta use cream and—aw," he said taking the milk from her. "I n-n-need some too. I'll just make us b-b-both some."

"Make that three?" Wyatt asked.

Gabby closed her eyes as he joined them. Why did he have to invade everything she did? She needed a second without him around.

He's what had kept her up all night. She couldn't believe Stephanie told him they'd been in Arkansas or that she'd left without telling him she was there. What no one knew was that she'd planned to tell him how she felt about him, and when she found him, a bunch of girls were hanging all over him. What chance did she have against them?

Family friend. Little kid. She couldn't compete against older girls, so she'd left without saying a word. And after dinner, he'd reminded her of exactly how he'd always see her. Family. Nothing more.

"Sure." Bandit said. "The more the merrier."

Wyatt chuckled. "Thanks. Is that okay with you?"

Opening her eyes, she lifted her gaze to his. Why was he always so good-looking? Or more like how? Tousled bed-head hair, dark cotton t-shirt, and draw-string pajama pants. He looked like he'd walked off a magazine page.

If she said anything other than sure, he'd want to know why, and she didn't want to give that answer. She shrugged a shoulder. "It's okay with me."

"Y-y-y'all take a seat in the living room, and I'll b-b-bring the hot chocolate out when they're done," Bandit said as he pulled out a large pot. "It sh-sh-shouldn't take too long."

"Thanks." Gabby slipped around Wyatt, hoping he'd want to stay in the kitchen and talk to Bandit.

Her hope was dashed when he sidled up beside her, smiling. "I thought I'd be the only one up this late, or I guess you could say early since it's after midnight. What's kept you from sleeping?"

Like she'd let that confession fly anytime soon. "I don't know. I guess I've just got a lot on my mind."

"Me too."

When they reached the living room, Gabby took a spot in the corner of the couch and curled her legs under her as she rubbed her arms. "It's a little chilly."

Wyatt walked to the fireplace. "I could get a fire going."

Pulling the blanket from the back of the couch, Gabby shook her head. "This will work."

"You think it's big enough for two? My feet are freezing."

Sharing a blanket with him? Life was just being unreasonably unfair since she'd returned home. "Uh…" Her brain wasn't fast enough.

He crossed the room, sat beside her, and pulled

part of the blanket over him. "Yeah, this blanket's plenty big enough."

It could be as large as Texas and not be big enough, but she was now trapped. "Guess it is."

"So, what's on your mind, keeping you up at night?"

"Oh, just stuff." Then she made the mistake of looking at him.

"What stuff? I mean, I know we weren't as tight as thieves like you and Carrie Anne were, but you can trust me." He smiled, and her gaze dipped to his lips.

With one little lift, her lips could touch his and her dreams of kissing him would be reality. Shortly followed by unfathomable embarrassment. How horrible would that be? It would take years to get over the awkwardness.

Wyatt bumped her shoulder with his. "Come on, spill."

"I'm thinking about moving back to Caprock Canyon." The words tumbled out before she could stop them. "I mean, of course, just thinking. Probably won't. It just…coming back home has me all nostalgic. That's all."

"I get it. I've been back a few times, and I've felt that way. It's hard to be away from home."

She nodded, and they sat in companionable silence

a second before her mouth began running again. "I think I might see if the old town newspaper is still up and running. If not, maybe I could see about starting it up again. Of course, I'd have to do some research. It may not be viable."

Taking a deep breath, Wyatt seemed to weigh what she'd said. "It couldn't hurt to try, that's for sure." He paused a second. "Hey, you want to go check out that pecan orchard later today to see if we want to get it going? After we've gotten some sleep? It could be fun. We'll just have to dress warmly. When I peeked outside, it hadn't snowed yet, but the weather app on my phone said to be expecting more. Maybe we can finally have an orchard like we talked about that summer."

"That might be tough. It's Thanksgiving Day. I don't know if we'll get the chance to do that." More importantly, she didn't want to be alone with him. She needed more time to get her head and heart on the same page: Wyatt was unavailable.

"We can't eat all day long."

"No, but you know we'll be playing cards at some point."

"I know. I was…how about the day after? We could go Friday."

Gabby shook her head. "I'm going with Carrie

Anne, my sister, and our moms to Amarillo to go Black Friday shopping."

His shoulders sagged. "Shopping?"

"You know, to get presents and stuff."

"How about after?"

"We'll probably be gone all day." Thank goodness, and she was genuinely thrilled until his lips turned down. Man, she hated how her insides melted when he looked sad. "Maybe we could go Saturday. Unless Carrie Anne has something planned."

His smile returned, and butterflies danced in her stomach. "I'll make sure she doesn't."

"O-o-okay," Bandit said as he walked into the living room. "They're d-d-done. Taste pretty g-g-good if I do say so myself." He handed Gabby and Wyatt a cup.

She wrapped her hands around it, letting the warmth seep through her fingers, and then brought it to her nose. Taking a deep breath, she closed her eyes. "It smells heavenly."

"Tt-th-thank you. It's my momma's recipe, b-b-bless her soul. The best c-c-cook ever."

Wyatt took a sip of his and winced. "I should've waited. This stuff is napalm."

Bandit laughed and sat in a chair adjacent to the couch. "It's just chocolate if it's n-n-not hot."

"Well, you've got the hot part down." Wyatt bent forward and set his cup on the coffee table. "I'll give it a second."

"I'd set mine down, but my hands are cold, and this feels good."

"So, w-w-what's g-g-got the two of you up at this time of night?" Bandit smiled as he took a sip of his drink. How he handled the temperature was beyond Gabby.

Wyatt crossed his arms over his chest. "Oh, just stuff on my mind." He hooked a thumb in her direction. "Same with her."

"W-w-what's on your mind, then?" Bandit asked.

Gabby lowered her cup to her lap. "I'm thinking about moving back home, but I'm not sure if that would work. Do you know if the Canyon Journal is still open?" It had been on its last leg when she'd left home.

"N-n-nah, it closed after you m-m-moved to Charleston. Mary Wise tried to keep it afloat, even going without p-p-pay, but Mr. Wise's health got t-t-to the point where she had to stop."

That saddened Gabby, but at the same time, it gave her ideas. She had a little money saved. If she got a loan at the bank and really worked hard, maybe she could restart it.

Chuckling, Wyatt smiled. "I can see the wheels turning a million miles a second."

"Hush. It's just thinking. As much as I'd like to, the reality is that I can't. I don't have the money to do that."

"I can help with that," Wyatt offered.

She shook her head. Never would she ever do that. The Wests weren't ATMs, and she wasn't taking a penny from them. "No. No way. I'm not taking money from you or anyone else."

Bandit nodded. "Yep, k-k-keep telling Bear the s-s-same thing. I won't take nothin' from h-h-him. He's m-m-my f-f-friend."

"What good is money if you can't share with the people you care about? You guys are like family to us. I don't get why it's such a big deal. Wouldn't you want to do the same?" Wyatt leaned forward and grabbed his mug, testing another sip. "Mmm. That's good stuff."

Like family. Again, there was that word. Before it could drag her down, she pushed it away and stayed on topic. Wyatt had a point about the money. If Gabby's family had won the lottery, they'd be trying to give it to the people they loved too. "Probably, but we didn't win, and we don't want to be the kind of people who only see you as dollar signs now. We don't want it ruining our friendships...our family."

"Exactly. If I take money, th-th-there'll eventually be the question of, was I a real friend or was I just st-st-sticking around for the money. Bear has been good to me. P-p-paying me to cook when he sure didn't have to."

"No, there would never be that question. We've been friends and family as long as we can remember. You two may not be blood, but you're as close as you can get."

Family. Friend. There they were again, like knives to the chest. Every time he spoke one, it felt like another nail in the coffin already riddled with them.

Gabby shrugged. "A restaurant for Bandit actually makes sense, but for me? Starting the paper up again makes no sense. Especially since the town is so small. People would come from all over for Bandit's cooking, but a paper? It's silly."

"The town is going to start growing now that the ranch is being revived. A paper would be great. You could talk about the history, why it's a great place to live, showcase what Bear did to this farmhouse." He paused a second. "We could start that orchard too. That could be a draw for people."

It was sweet and wonderful and impossible. There was no way her heart could handle being around Wyatt every day and not get to be with him. She'd have front row seats to watch him date and fall in love with someone else, and it was more than she could handle. It was practically a nightmare to even think about it.

Bandit stood. "Y-y-you two keep talking. I'm g-g-gonna catch a few winks before I have to get d-d-dinner going." With that, Bandit downed his hot chocolate and left.

Wyatt twisted in the seat to face Gabby. "I'm serious. I'd love to help you get the paper going again."

Gabby shook her head. "Wyatt, no. I'm going back to Charleston. You're going back to the rodeo. That's your first love. This other stuff would just get in your way."

His shoulders sagged. "Yeah, I guess you're right."

The silence stretched out between them, making the house feel eerily quiet.

Clearing his throat, Wyatt said, "Can I ask you a question?"

"Sure."

He lifted his gaze to hers, an unreadable expression on his face. "You wouldn't be disappointed in me if I quit, would you?"

"Bull riding?" If he was thinking of quitting, she'd be floored.

"Yeah," he whispered.

Whoa. This was big. "You've always loved doing it. I can't even picture you not on a bull, but I'd never be disappointed in you. No one would."

"You sure?"

"Positive."

A small smile quirked on his lips, and he covered her hand with his, making her skin tingle. His lips were too close and kissable. She tried to pull free, but he held on to her hand. "You came to all my events?"

Her expression softened. "I thought you needed someone there."

He tilted his head as his eyebrows knitted together. "Then why didn't you let me know you were there?"

Why? Because it wasn't long after seeing him with all those girls that Lori stepped into the picture. For a while, Gabby held on to hope that he'd see she was just using him, but that never happened. They'd break up, and it felt like seconds later that they were back together.

The last event she went to, she'd found enough courage to tell him how she felt, only to find him lip-locked with Lori. They'd broken up, he'd said, for good, but there Lori was...all over him. It had broken her heart. That was the day Gabby had put feelers out for other colleges.

And then the final straw that sent her packing was the summer before her sophomore year...him asking Lori to marry him. But it was pointless to even talk about it.

"I..." She slipped from his grip and stood. "I should get to bed. So should you."

He jumped up with her and took her by the arms. "What aren't you telling me?"

Cripes. She needed to get some distance. "It's water under the bridge." This time when she pulled free, she took off for the stairs as quickly as she could, not stopping until she was in the safety of her room.

Crawling into bed, she curled on her side and quietly wished she'd stayed in Charleston. Nothing she said would make Wyatt see her any different. No, it was better for both of them if she kept her lips locked and her feelings to herself. As much as she tried to tell herself she was over Wyatt, she wasn't.

New Year's Eve. Not that far away at all. She could keep it together until then. Maybe.

CHAPTER 8

ontinuously checking the clock wasn't working for Wyatt. It was much like waiting for water to boil. The more he checked it, the longer it took for the girls to get back home. Surely, they'd be home any second. How much Black Friday shopping could they do? Were they buying the store?

He needed to talk to Gabby. After their middle-of-the-night conversation, he'd been desperate to find out why she'd run off. He'd spent all of Thanksgiving Day trying to get her alone so they could talk, but it seemed she was deliberately avoiding him. He couldn't for the life of him figure out what he'd done to make her bolt like that.

After all this time, he'd found out she'd been to all

his events, even the one in Arkansas. Why hadn't she ever let him know? It would have made his day to know family was with him. She'd looked so...upset when he'd asked her about it. Her lips had turned down, and there was a sadness to her voice he'd never heard before. It made no sense to him.

When the sound of his mom's diesel Excursion rumbled outside, he couldn't get to the door fast enough. They'd taken it to make sure they had enough room for everything. He couldn't imagine them *needing* all that room, but again, women were strange creatures. They did things all the time that baffled him.

He grabbed his coat from the hook and pushed his arms through the sleeves as he jogged down the front steps and stopped next to Gabby. "Did ya'll have fun?"

"Yeah, I had fun," Gabby said through a yawn as she got out of the car.

"I can help bring in stuff," he offered.

Carrie Anne bounced over to him and hugged his bicep. "That's very sweet, big brother, but then you'd see your gifts. You'll ruin the surprise."

A grin stretched on his lips. "I won't peek."

His sister eyed him. "You're as bad as Josiah when it comes to sneaking and peeking."

THE BEST FRIEND'S BILLIONAIRE BROTHER

He chuckled. "I'll be good this time, Scout's honor."

Carrie Anne shook her head. "We've got it."

He looked at Gabby. "You trust me, doncha?"

She hugged herself. "Not with presents."

His mouth dropped open. "Where is the love, people?"

The back of the SUV opened, and his mom peeked from around the back. "Wyatt, go on in the house. We've got this."

Wyatt scoffed. "Aw, you don't trust me either?"

"Not as far as I can throw you. Get!" She pointed at the house.

His sister took Gabby's hand. "We'll get yours too if you want to go lie down."

He turned his attention to Gabby. "Is something wrong?"

Stephanie walked up to them and stopped. "It got hot in the car, and she's been a little sick to her stomach."

"I can manage my own bags," Gabby said.

Now that Wyatt was really paying attention, her color was off, and her eyes weren't nearly as bright as usual. Unlike when he picked her up from the airport, she'd probably forgotten to take something for her carsickness this time. It bothered him that she wasn't feeling good. "I can get you something fizzy. It would probably help your stomach."

She gave him a weak smile. "I'll be okay. I'm feeling better."

"I owe you for that time I had my tonsils out."

Carrie Anne looked from Gabby to Wyatt. "What time?"

"Right after twelfth grade. Remember? I kept getting strep."

His sister's eyebrows knitted together. "Oh, right. I'd gone to camp. Gabby and I went every summer. I hadn't remembered the excuse...but she didn't go that year."

All Wyatt could remember was that she'd kept him company after his surgery. It hadn't even dawned on him at the time that she should've been at camp. "You were supposed to go to camp that week?"

"Um...I..." Gabby set her hand over her stomach. "I'm going to lie down so I can rest before we put the tree up. I'll see you guys later."

"Wait..." He started to go after her, when Carrie Anne held him back. Returning his attention to her, he scrunched his eyebrows together. "Why didn't you let me go after her?"

"Because I have a few questions for you."

"Couldn't they wait until I see if she's okay?" His voice rose an octave on the last word.

His sister dropped her hands from his bicep and crossed her arms over her chest. "Wyatt, you are about as thick as they come, so I'm going to use small words and talk slowly, okay?"

"I'm not stupid." Carrie Anne was frustrating the tar out of him. All this talk of him being dumb and thick. He was no such thing.

"How many times did Gabby and I go to camp?"

Shrugging he said, "I dunno, every year since the moment you were old enough."

"Okay, and each time we went, we came back and we were..." She let the sentence travel off as she waved her hand, indicating she was waiting for him to finish the sentence.

"You loved it."

"So...Gabby misses a camp that she's gone to year after year, something she loves, to stay here...and what does she do that week instead?"

His sister was reading way too much into things. "Her parents had planned a trip, and it fell through. They'd forgotten it was camp week when they planned it."

Carrie Anne palmed her forehead as she sighed. "Oh, Wyatt...what am I going to do with you?"

"Carrie Anne, I have no idea what you're talking about. Gabby is like a sister to me. We're just good friends. That's all. She hung out with me that week because Mom didn't want to leave me alone. I mean, I sure wasn't anything exciting."

"Oh my stars." She dropped her hand from her forehead. "She likes you, Wyatt. She has since we were kids. I've never said anything before this because I thought you'd eventually figure it out."

He set his hands on his hips and cast his gaze to the ground. "You're reading way too much into this. Gabby doesn't think of me like that."

"Except, she does. Why else would she go to all your events?"

"Because that's what friends do. Friends who are more like family. You support each other."

With another big sigh as she shook her head, she said, "That's true, but have you asked yourself why she went to all your rodeo events but didn't even let you know she was there?"

No, he'd not figured that out. He'd wanted to, but how could he when he could never get Gabby alone? "Not yet. Do you know?"

Carrie Anne held his gaze. "Because each time after you rode, she'd go looking for you, only to find girls hanging all over you."

"What does that have to do with her never letting me know she was there?"

His sister threw her hands up. "You're hopeless." She turned to walk away and stopped. "One of these days, you're going to figure out the real answer to that question, and she'll have moved on. You're going to wake up one day and realize you've lost her. You should spend some time simmering on that thought for a bit." With that, she walked to the back of the car to unload gifts, leaving Wyatt with a lot to think about.

Lose Gabby? That wasn't possible. They were family. Her meeting someone wouldn't change that. Although, now that he was really chewing on it, it bugged him. A lot more than he cared to admit. Gabby with another man? The thought made the hair on the back of his neck stand up. She had said she was supposedly dating someone in Charleston, but Carrie Anne talked like it wasn't true.

He closed his eyes and took a deep breath. Why was he even going down that road? Carrie Anne and her meddling. That was all this was. She just didn't understand the nature of his friendship with Gabby. They'd always been there for each other. That's the way they operated.

Frustrated, he grumbled as he strode back inside the house. Gabby's laughter filtered from the kitchen, and curiosity propelled him to find the source of it. At the entry, he froze.

Gabby was giggling like a schoolgirl, and Bandit had a huge smile on his face. She touched his arm, and he pulled her into a hug. "Oh, s-s-sweetheart, I m-m-missed you."

"I've missed you too."

Bandit leaned back, kissed her on the forehead, and hugged her again. "You c-c-can't stay gone so l-l-long this time."

Wyatt cast his gaze to the floor, feeling like he'd walked in on something he wasn't supposed to see. Was there something going on between Gabby and Bandit? And why did it bug him to even think about it? It made him even more frustrated with Carrie Anne.

Lifting his gaze, he cleared his throat, and Gabby and Bandit looked over at him. "Hey, W-W-Wyatt," Bandit said.

"Hey. I thought you weren't feeling good." Wyatt directed the question to Gabby.

"I was just getting something to drink before I went to my room."

He held her gaze. "I think you were doing more than getting a drink." Where had that come from, and why was he suddenly mad?

Her eyebrows knitted together. "And if I was, what business is it of yours? I don't answer to you. I'm just a family friend, right?" She looked at Bandit. "Thank you for the drink." She kissed his cheek and stormed past Wyatt. Her footsteps could be heard all the way to her room.

Bandit lifted an eyebrow. "S-s-something wrong, Wyatt?"

"No," he huffed. "Nothing's wrong. Just...I didn't know you two were an item."

"You didn't?" Carrie Anne asked.

He'd been so caught up in watching Bandit and Gabby that he hadn't heard Carrie Anne come inside. Turning to her, he said, "They're an item?" Hadn't she just made a big deal about Gabby liking him? "I thought she was dating a guy named Tim."

"She told me they'd just started talking." Carrie Anne shrugged. "If you snooze, you lose, big brother. I told you that outside. I guess I just didn't realize how serious they were."

Wyatt's stomach dropped to his boots. "You got me all twisted up. I told you Gabby was family, and this just proves it." Heat rushed up his neck to the tips of his ears.

"Then why are you so mad?" She smiled as she tilted her head.

"I'm not. I'm perfectly fine." He swore under his breath. His sister was pushing every button he had. It was just like her, too. She'd done it all the time when they were kids. "I'm going to my room. You're just... just..." He waved her off and stormed to his room.

He stopped as he shut his bedroom door, fuming. He wasn't mad that Gabby and Bandit were together. He was mad that no one told him. That Carrie Anne was making him think all sorts of things that obviously weren't true.

Wyatt shook his head, crossed the room, and put his head in his hands as he sat on the edge of his bed. *You're going to wake up one day and realize you've lost her.* Carrie Anne's words floated to mind. Would he be upset if Gabby found someone to love? A someone that wasn't him?

A few minutes ago, he'd had a solid answer, but now he wasn't so sure. It was all his sister's fault that he was so mixed up. What could he do? Or the better question was, what was he going to do? His career, his love life, and everything in between seemed so out of control lately. Coming home was supposed to help, not further complicate things.

Dropping back on the bed, he slammed his fist down on the mattress and stared at the ceiling. "I don't know what to do. If anyone's listening, I sure could use some help."

Wyatt sure hoped someone was listening because he needed a heaping dose of help, and now. His world was getting more and more confusing. His problems were turning into round holes, and all he had were square pegs. If something didn't find a way to fit and soon, he wasn't sure what he was going to do.

CHAPTER 9

"Go away, Wyatt!" Gabby yelled through her bedroom door as she leaned against it. What right did he have to question who she spent time with?

"It's Carrie Anne."

Could she have just one break? Just one where she wasn't feeling like a ship being thrown against rocks. "I don't want to talk about it."

"Yeah, you do," Carrie Anne said softly. "My brother has a brain the size of a walnut, and it's half-cracked."

After crossing the room, Gabby crawled onto her bed and curled her legs under her. "No, I don't."

Carrie Anne entered the room and sat beside Gabby on the bed. "He was jealous."

Of course, Gabby's heart wanted to believe that. He'd sure looked jealous. He'd been red-faced when she stormed away, but her head knew the score. She'd learned long ago that reading into Wyatt's actions or words often led to disappointment.

"He was caught off guard. He knows good and well that Bandit and I aren't an item. I love the guy, but there's no spark there at all. Believe me, I wish there was." Gabby grabbed a pillow and hugged it to her.

"I understand not wanting to get your hopes up, but he was absolutely beside himself. He was *not* okay with the idea that you and Bandit might be together." Carrie Anne paused and chewed her lip.

It was a Carrie Anne tell. That look was the one she made when she'd done something she shouldn't have. "What? What did you do?"

The silence stretched until Gabby couldn't stand it. "Carrie Anne, what did you do?"

"I told Wyatt you liked him."

Gabby's lips parted in a gasp. "You didn't."

Nodding, Carrie Anne winced. "He needed to know. I love my brother, but that boy could wave a red flag in front of a bull and wonder why it charged him. He's not dumb, just wholly and completely clueless."

A laugh popped out of Gabby. It was true. Wyatt was adorably goofy sometimes. Not that he was trying to be. He just...sometimes, he could hit a tree and wonder how that forest got there. "Okay, so you might be right about that."

"Gabby, I love you, and I love Wyatt. I know somewhere in that brain of his, the net is just waiting to catch a clue. He just needs...a little help getting there. So, I have an idea."

Squeezing her eyes shut, Gabby's stomach somersaulted. "Oh no." She opened her eyes. "No ideas. I mean...you had an idea to spy on Hank Clines because you thought he stole your Barbie Jeep. We both ended up with a broken arm because the tree branch broke."

Carrie Anne gasped. "That wasn't my fault! You ate all those cookies!"

Leveling her eyes at Carrie Anne, she said, "We both got poison ivy when you decided it would be a great idea to get a picture of the huge black bear when we went camping in Colorado."

Carrie Anne scoffed. "I swear it was a bear."

"It was a rabbit."

Shaking her head, Carrie Anne shrugged. "We were going into high school. I needed a good picture to get on the newspaper team with you. So, technically, that was your fault."

"It was not!" Gabby sighed and shook her head. "My point is that you have ideas and they usually end up with us in pain." She could only imagine the pain she'd be in if Carrie Anne's idea included Wyatt.

"It'll work. I know it will."

Gabby rolled her eyes. "You're not going to quit until you get it out, are you?"

Shaking her head, Carrie Anne grinned. "Nope."

"Fine. What's your idea?"

Her friend giggled and bounced on the bed. "Okay, so…we'll need Bandit in on this, but I think we can do it."

Closing her eyes, Gabby wilted. "I don't like where this is going."

A smile spread on Carrie Anne's lips. "We make Wyatt think you and Bandit are serious."

"No," Gabby said. "No way."

"It'll work!"

Gabby groaned and palmed her forehead. "It'll be a colossal failure, and I'll be the one with a broken heart. This isn't going to work." She'd almost said she just needed to get over Wyatt. With that revelation, Carrie Anne would've been rabid.

"Please, just try it. Just…I don't know, try to plan for the worst and hope for the best. You know, just, if it works, it works, and if it doesn't, you go back to South Carolina knowing once and for all that it's over." Carrie Anne took Gabby's hand in hers. "I know this will be hard, but I really think it'll work."

Silence settled over them as Gabby considered the crazy idea. It had disaster written all over it, but that tiny voice that whispered, *What if*, reared its ugly head. What if it worked? What if Wyatt's eyes were finally opened? Could they have a relationship, and would it work out?

"Come on, Gabby, I'll never push it again as long as I live if this doesn't work."

"Okay." Okay? Holy smokes. "I mean—"

Carrie Anne let go of Gabby's hand and grinned. "Nope. I'm not letting you back out." She took a deep breath and released it. "So, we just need to talk to Bandit."

Gabby rolled her eyes. "Fine, but if he doesn't want to participate in this little scheme, it's over."

"I accept your terms." She jumped up. "I'll be right back."

As Carrie Anne slipped out of her room, Gabby let out a frustrated breath. No way was this going to work, because there was no way Bandit would agree to Carrie Anne's scheme. The man was too smart for that. At least, Gabby hoped he was.

Wyatt wasn't jealous; he was nosey. He hated it when

he was the last to find something out. He'd been furious when she announced she was leaving for South Carolina. It had taken seconds, and he was over it, which just provided further proof that he wasn't interested in her.

The door to her room opened, and Carrie Anne slipped inside with Bandit.

"O-o-okay, why d-d-did you need to talk to m-m-me?" Bandit asked.

Carrie Anne crossed the room and sat on the edge of the bed. "We need a favor."

His eyes narrowed. "A f-f-favor?"

"We need you to pretend you're Gabby's boyfriend."

Bandit's eyes widened. He looked from Carrie Anne to Gabby and back. "Uh, wh-what?"

Gabby held back a laugh. "See, even he thinks it's a horrible plan."

"Shush, you!" Carrie Anne hissed. "Wyatt needs to think you are dating Gabby. We—"

"Whatchoo mean, 'we'?" Gabby cut her off.

With a pop to the arm, Carrie Anne continued. "We want to make Wyatt jealous so he'll finally realize Gabby is more to him than family or friend."

Bandit set his hands on his hips. "Y-y-you also thought it was a g-g-great idea t-t-that I set Bear up on a f-f-farmer's dating w-w-website."

Gabby gasped. "Carrie Anne, you didn't!"

"What? I've found the love of my life. Is it really all that wrong to want my brothers to find love?"

"But a dating website? Really?" Gabby pinched the bridge of her nose. "You're incorrigible." She looked at Carrie Anne. "He's going to kill you when he finds out." She cut an eye toward Bandit. "And you too."

He shrugged. "I-I-I haven't f-f-finished it yet."

"What?" Carrie Anne huffed. "You said you were almost done last night."

"I-I-I said I thought I c-c-could finish. B-b-bear walked in on me, and I had to s-s-stop."

"Okay, I'll help you finish it up after this." Carrie Anne grumbled under her breath. "Back to Gabby and Wyatt. Would you help us?"

When Bandit didn't immediately respond, Carrie Anne stood and walked to him, taking his hand. "Please, Bandit, you're our only hope."

Gabby rolled her eyes. "You are *not* Princess Leia."

Waving her off, Carrie Anne worked her puppy dog eyes. "Please."

He pointed at her face. "Th-th-that's not f-f-fair. Y-y-you stop that!"

"Please."

As he took a big breath, he closed his eyes. "I'm g-g-goin' to regret this, but a-a-all right."

Carrie Anne squealed and hugged him around the neck, kissing his cheek. "You are the best, Bandit! Just the absolute best!"

Gabby wilted sideways on the bed. "We're both doomed."

More than doomed. It would be all kinds of painful, but it would also mean Gabby was done wishing and hoping and pining. Wyatt would be a past crush, and Gabby would have to face that reality. As much as she'd tried to convince herself that she was over Wyatt, she wasn't. Maybe Carrie Anne's hare-brained idea would help Gabby move on once and for all.

Then she could look to the future with a sharper focus. With Bear starting the ranch again, Caprock Canyon would have people coming back. They'd need a newspaper. Gabby could have the best of both worlds. She could have her family and her career.

She sure had missed home. The day spent shopping had made her realize just how much, too. Her mom and sister laughing and teasing. Carrie Anne talking a mile a minute about everything from what she was getting Israel for their wedding to the names they were debating for their first child. She'd missed Mrs. West too—how much her relationship with Gabby's mom resembled Carrie Anne's and Gabby's.

Staying away from her home because she wanted something she couldn't have was ridiculous. The time away, on her own, had helped her grow up and taught her to face her challenges, and deal with life when it handed her lemons. Like thinking she was getting a promotion when she was actually being let go. Yes, it hurt, but she wasn't crushed, and she didn't need to let her infatuation with Wyatt crush her either. She couldn't let him keep her away from home any longer.

The bed moved as Carrie Anne sat down again, going over her plan with Bandit. "Okay, so, you'll plan things with Gabby and either be hung up with something or just not show up. I'll make sure Wyatt knows about them and see that he's the one filling in."

"Carrie Anne, I s-s-sure hope you know what you're d-d-doing. If he really gets j-j-jealous, he'll knock m-m-my lights out."

Gabby used her hand and pushed herself back up. "That's not going to happen because he's not jealous. You know how he gets when he thinks he's been left out of the loop. That's all that was earlier."

"Hush," Carrie Anne said. "That's not what it was."

"Was too." Gabby pinched her lips together. "I can be just as stubborn as you are."

Bandit held up his hands. "Ladies, j-j-just tell me what to do, and we'll g-g-get this plan in m-m-motion.

If he knocks my t-t-teeth loose, you're p-p-paying for the dentist, Carrie Anne."

"I'll get you the best set of false teeth this state's ever seen." She winked.

Bandit gave her one last look and left, mumbling something about women and weird.

Carrie Anne faced Gabby. "Okay, so let's talk strategy."

Gabby shoulders sagged. It was more like *stragedy*...a strategy of tragedy. Doomed. This whole thing was doomed.

CHAPTER 10

arefoot and still in pajamas, Wyatt slowly walked into the kitchen, rubbing his eyes. He'd struggled to go to sleep after watching Gabby and Bandit being all snuggly with each other the evening before. Add to it all the talk of feelings about Gabby. Plus, he was still trying to decide if he wanted his rodeo career back. It was enough to drive him bonkers.

"B-b-breakfast is about over," Bandit said with a laugh.

"I'm not hungry." Wyatt's irk flag was already at half-mast, and Bandit hadn't done anything wrong. "I'm sorry. I didn't sleep well. You got any coffee left?"

Bandit took a cup from one of the cabinets and handed it to him. "Pot's got a l-l-little left."

"Thanks." Wyatt poured the last of what remained into his mug and took a seat at the kitchen island. He took a tentative sip and then a big drink. "This is good."

"M-m-mom's recipe. It's n-n-not bitter."

Not even a little. On the road, Wyatt had choked down his fair share of coffee so nasty sugar couldn't save it. "You know, you really should open a restaurant. I know you don't want to take money from us, but with Bear getting this place going again, townfolk are going to need a place to go. Why not yours? You're the best cook I've ever known."

Bandit shook his head. "No."

"Bear said he'd even do a contract. Charge you interest if it would make you feel better." Wyatt set his cup on the counter. "What good is all this money if we can't share it? You're family, Bandit. Just 'cause you didn't claim it with us doesn't make it any less so." Oh, they'd tried to get him to take a share of the winnings, but just like his parents and the Fredericks, Bandit wouldn't have any of it.

"It's th-th-the principle of it." His lips curved up. "Hey, s-s-sweetheart!"

Wyatt followed his line of sight. Of course, it was Gabby, dressed in curve-hugging jeans and a red turtleneck sweater. Her hair was pulled up with the tips of it grazing her shoulders. Mercy, she was breathtaking. Her eyes twinkled, and her skin glowed. Why, he didn't even need coffee to perk up after all.

"Hey, are you almost ready?" she asked as she crossed the kitchen and hugged Bandit, kissing his cheek.

Now Wyatt's blood was boiling. His half-mast irk was waving like a sheet in a tornado, one clothesline clip away from being ripped off. "Ready? Ready for what?"

"Oh, hey, Wyatt."

Oh, hey, Wyatt? Like she didn't see him sitting there? "We're supposed to go look at the orchard today."

She looked up at Bandit. "I'd totally forgotten about that."

Bandit tapped her nose with his index finger. "It's o-o-okay 'cause you're c-c-cute."

Her cheeks turned a hue of rosy pink that bugged Wyatt. Why didn't she blush like that when he complimented her? He picked up his cup, took a big swig, and stood. "I guess I'll go by myself."

"W-w-why don't you go a-a-ahead and go with Wyatt to see that orchard." He paused. "Mrs. West was in h-h-here earlier, and she wanted to go over a f-f-few things for Carrie Anne's wedding since I'm d-d-doing the c-c-cooking."

The way Wyatt's heart thrummed against his ribs, he'd have thought he'd won the lottery again. There'd be none of that infuriating canoodling if she and Bandit weren't together.

Wyatt hung his head as shame filled him. Gabby deserved to be happy, even if that meant Bandit and not him.

The last bit of that thought caught him off guard as he chugged the rest of his coffee, and he choked. He held his chest with his hand and worked to keep coffee from shooting out his nose like Old Faithful at Yellowstone. Where on earth had that idea come from?

"Are you okay, Wyatt?" Gabby asked as she approached him with a kitchen towel in hand.

He took the towel and held it over his mouth until he could catch his breath. "I'm fine." And he was until he locked eyes with her. Fine flitted out the window and blew down the street. He wasn't fine at all.

She palmed his cheek. "Are you sure? That sounded like it hurt."

"No…I mean, yeah, I'm okay," he said, his voice thick. "If you have plans, we can see the orchard another day."

Looking over her shoulder, she smiled. "I appreciate the thoughtfulness, but Carrie Anne's wedding takes priority over my dating life."

Dating life. Dating Bandit. His mind and his heart screamed it was all wrong. She shouldn't be dating Bandit. The man was family, but he wasn't the right guy for Gabby. "Okay, I guess I'll go get ready."

"Okay." She left Wyatt and returned to Bandit, whispering something Wyatt couldn't make out.

On the way out of the kitchen, he looked over his shoulder, and his chest constricted. Gabby's little nose had scrunched up as she giggled at whatever Bandit whispered back. Wyatt had loved when she'd done that when they were younger, so much so that there were times when he'd goof around just to see her laugh like that. What would it take for her to do that for Wyatt again? Lord have mercy. It was as earnest a plea as he'd ever had. All these weird feelings needed to just go away.

Now it felt like his time with her was over, or at least the way they used to be. Wyatt couldn't be the guy who made her laugh or seek her out when he had a problem. Not like he used to do. If she was with Bandit, everything would be different.

All that too-late talk was the problem. His sister

putting ideas in his head. Still, her neon words were breaking the dam and flooding his brain. *Too late...*

Wyatt shook his head, trying to clear his wayward thoughts. It was wrong to even entertain thoughts of stepping between her and Bandit. The guy was family, and so was Gabby. No, Wyatt needed to respect them and be happy for them. That was the right thing to do.

It was time for a shower and then exploring the orchard with a friend, and only a friend. That's what his head said, but his heart was singing a different tune. One that was off-key, sounding like a tomcat. He rubbed his face with his hands and groaned. Why did all this stuff have to be so complicated?

When an answer didn't come, he headed for the shower, hoping hot water and quiet would help ease the war going on in his mind.

GLANCING AT GABBY, Wyatt tried to think of a way to start a conversation. It wasn't nearly as hard before he found out she was dating Bandit. Leave it to his sister to muck with things that were perfectly fine the way they were.

"Why do you keep staring at me?" Gabby asked.

He startled, and the truck swerved a little. "What?"

Gabby grabbed the dash and squeaked. "What is wrong with you this morning?"

He took a deep breath as he focused on the road ahead. "Nothing's wrong with me. Is something wrong with you?"

"You've been acting weird since breakfast."

"Have not. I just didn't sleep well last night, and..." What could he say? That finding out her new relationship status with Bandit had hit him wrong? He sure couldn't answer the inevitable "why" if he did.

She twisted in the seat and crossed her arms over her chest. "You've been grumbling since your feet hit the first floor after your shower, and now you're staring at me and trying to put us in a ditch. What is going on?"

"I didn't know you were dating Bandit." It slipped out so fast that Wyatt was blindsided.

Her eyebrows knitted together. "Why would you care?"

"I don't."

"Then what else are you upset about?"

He cut a glance at her. "I'm not upset."

Dropping her hands to her lap, she took a deep breath and tucked a piece of hair behind her ear. "You are too. I'm sorry you were the last to find out. It's always bothered you."

"I'm not bothered. Just…" He scratched the back of his neck. "I just didn't know you thought of Bandit that way."

"Why not? He's a good guy."

"I don't know. I guess I pictured you dating someone different."

"Like who?"

Shrugging, he tried to think of an answer. "I…"

Gabby's eyebrows drew together. "Did you think I'd stay single forever? Or is it that you can't stop seeing me as a little kid?"

Now that she was asking, he hadn't really thought about it at all. Her dating someone had never even crossed his mind. Why hadn't it, though? She was a beautiful woman. Intelligent, caring, warm, and wonderful. Honestly, she'd always been one of his closest friends. The person he trusted with all his secrets. But he'd never considered another man enjoying her company.

Of course, he'd thought of *her* while she was gone. Felt her absence. Missed her smile and her laughter. How comfortable he was when he was with her.

When she'd first announced she was leaving for South Carolina, it had taken him off guard, gutting

THE BEST FRIEND'S BILLIONAIRE BROTHER

him, since she'd stuck close to home until then. At the time, he'd chalked it up to not liking change, but soon after, he'd realized it was that he didn't like her living so far away. She was another fixture in the family like anyone else.

"Well?" she asked, pausing a beat before adding, "You thought I'd never date, didn't you? When I left for South Carolina, you'd asked Lori to marry you. Did you think you were the only one allowed to have a future with someone?"

"No, and..."

"I'm not the same little girl you teased as a kid."

"I know that," he huffed.

Of all the things that were true, that was the truest. Gabby was very much a grown woman. Not just gorgeous, but someone he enjoyed being with, kid sister's best friend or not. And despite his effort to ignore what his sister had said, he'd been simmering on her words more that he liked to admit. Especially sitting this close to Gabby. He was most definitely not seeing her as a little kid. Not by a long shot.

He took a deep breath. "No, of all the people in the world, you deserve to be happy. If Bandit gives you that, then I'm all for it." That's what his lips said, but for the first time since coming home, his heart and his head were on the same page. Wyatt wanted Gabby to be happy...but with him.

The thought slammed into his chest like a battering ram, hitting with such a force, he was winded. *Too late*...whispered in the back of his mind again. He didn't want to be that guy, but the idea of losing Gabby ate him up.

What was he going to do now? She was dating his friend. A guy that was more family than anything. Trying to come between Bandit and Gabby would be like stabbing a brother in the back. It wasn't honorable. It wasn't right. How could he fix all this?

"I'm sorry, Gabby," he said and took her hand. "I didn't mean for it to come out like that or to make you mad."

Squeezing his hand, she smiled. "I know. Bandit and I have just started talking. That's it. I enjoy his company."

Man, that hurt Wyatt's heart to hear. Not that she was happy, but that she was happy with another man. A guy that he respected and thought of as a brother. But they were only talking. That was good news, right?

"I thought you were dating Tim, anyway." He raised an eyebrow.

A pink blush swept over Gabby's cheeks, and she

bit her lip. "There is no Tim. I had to do something to try to tamp down Carrie Anne's meddling in my love life." She sighed. "She thinks she needs to find everyone's love since she's found hers."

Wyatt laughed. "Tell me about it. She just can't help herself."

They were quiet for a few more minutes before he broke the silence.

"Why didn't you ever tell me you were at my events?" He glanced at her, watching for her expression.

She blinked, and her lips parted.

"I want the truth."

Twisting in the seat, she faced forward again. "I think that's water under the bridge."

The house belonging to the orchard came into view, and he slowed the pickup down. "Well, that bridge is rickety and can't hold any weight. I want to know why."

She turned away from him. "Because every time I came to say hi, you had girls all over you."

Wyatt parked the truck in front of the house and cut the engine. "Why would that have stopped you? They were just...girls. You're family. That's always been more important."

With a small nod of her head, she replied softly,

"Yeah, you're right. I should have let you know." She cleared her throat. "We should probably check out the orchard. Bandit and I have plans tonight." She quickly opened the door and jumped out of the truck.

Why did it sound like she was on the verge of tears? All he'd done was ask a simple question. There was no need to be upset about it.

He shook his head. He was probably reading too much into it. Carrie Anne clearly didn't know what she was talking about anyway.

He got out of the pickup and joined Gabby at the front. "I didn't mean to upset you." He pulled her into a hug. "I'm sorry. I just…I wish I'd known. What I was trying to say was that you're more important than a bunch of girls."

"It's okay. I can be too sensitive sometimes." She set her forehead against his chest and wrapped her arms around his waist. "I'm sorry too." She looked up at him.

His heart skipped a beat and then hit marathon speed. He liked the feel of her in his arms. While they might not have been completely joined at the hip as kids, they were good friends. There had been a few times he'd gone looking for Carrie Anne, only to catch Gabby instead. She'd given him girl advice every so often.

Then there was the time he'd had his tonsils out when she'd stayed with him that whole week. At the time, he thought nothing of it. With the revelation that Gabby had skipped a summer camp she loved in order to be with him, it changed how he saw their entire history. On the surface, he'd always thought of her as family, but digging a little deeper...he was seeing that things weren't as black and white now.

Gabby dropped her arms and stepped back. "I guess we should check out the house."

He nodded, but his thoughts were jumbled. His whole world had been flipped on its head, and he didn't know how to right it. All these feelings were probably off anyway. Carrie Anne had planted seeds of doubt, and his mind was letting them grow. That made more sense than anything.

Turning, he faced the house and shook his head to clear his thoughts. He needed to concentrate on why they were at the orchard. Now that his attention was focused on the house, a rush of excitement hit him as his mind began going a million miles a minute. Lately, bull riding didn't even give him this feeling.

This place was full of potential, and he was sure Bear would let them buy this part of the ranch from him. It would take a ton of work, but there was a full-color picture of the finished product playing in his mind like a big screen at a drive-in. A little blood, a lot of sweat, and a bucket of tears, and this old house could be a fantastic place to hang his hat. He and Gabby could make this happen, just like they'd talked about years before.

CHAPTER 11

*A*s Gabby rubbed her arms, she studied the house while trying to squelch the ache in her heart. Family. Even after talking about her not being a little kid anymore. He still didn't think of her as anything else. If she thought actually spelling it out would help, she would, but not with the puzzled way he'd looked at her when she'd mentioned all the girls hanging on him. What would be the point?

She felt Wyatt's presence next to her and stuffed her hands in her pockets. "Boy, it sure is a mess."

"Yeah, the years haven't been kind to it."

"Nope."

The one-story ranch-style home had been beautiful...at one point. It was mostly brick, with chipped white paint accents. The wrap-around porch, railing, and steps had been stained at one point, but now they were weathered. The roof was missing half its shingles, leading Gabby to think the interior was a mess. Restoring this home would be a serious project.

Why was she even considering it? A project with a man who only thought of her as family would be torture. Besides, all those talks about an orchard were just ramblings of a lovesick girl and a tonsil-less guy.

"Wanna check out the inside?" Gabby smiled and looked at him. "I hope the bones are still good, but I'm not holding my breath."

Nodding, his gaze roamed from one side of the house to the other and then landed on her. "Me either."

She nearly gulped. To her, he was the best-looking guy no matter who was in the room, but today he'd somehow managed to crank that up a notch. The way his jacket collar was pulled up, framing his jaw with his dark blue button-up check shirt peeking out, he was breathtaking.

"Okay, let's check it out." She pulled her gaze from his and tucked her head down as she reached the steps leading to the house.

Two steps up, she heard a snap before her boot went through it. Waving her arms wildly, she tried to keep herself from falling; the next thing she knew, Wyatt's arms were around her.

"Whoa," he said, holding her to him. "I guess we'll mark that on the to-do list."

Her hammering heart and shaky nerves kept her from speaking, so she nodded.

He pulled her boot out of the step and set her on the ground. "Hey, it's okay. Are you hurt?"

Part of her screamed to pretend it was broken so he'd have to carry her, but the more logical part won out. "I don't think so. It hurts a little, but I think that's just from my boot falling through."

"You sure?" he asked as he kept his hold on her.

Stepping back, she nodded and said, "Yeah. At least you know what step to avoid." She laughed, her nerves making her voice sound shaky.

Using his long legs, Wyatt stepped over the second step, onto the third, and then to the porch. He took a few tentative steps and then offered her his hand. "I think the porch is okay."

Gabby took it, ignoring the tingles, and set her foot on the first step, letting him pull her up. "I should have been more careful."

"Eh, it can happen to anybody."

"I know, but I feel a little silly now." Then she realized he was still holding her hand and pulled it free.

"Time to see the house." She took a few steps and tried the door.

It swung open, and sure enough, the ceiling was partially caved in. The large living room had once been painted a soft buttery yellow, but with rain getting in, it now had sheetrock peeling off. Several planks of the wood floor were curled up.

Shaking her head, she said, "Oh, wow. This is…" She took a deep breath. "A mess. This will take a while to fix."

"Yeah, it sure will."

"You think it's safe to walk through the rest of the house?" She turned to face him.

He shrugged. "I don't know, but I don't think we should risk it. Let's try the back door. Most of the roof damage looked to be concentrated in this room. Maybe it's not so bad everywhere else."

Gabby nodded, and they slowly made their way around the porch, checking the decking as they went. As they rounded the corner, they stopped. "Well, so far so good. At least the deck has held," she said.

Wyatt nodded. "For the most part. Could be that step that broke was already weak from before the house was abandoned."

They continued to the back door, which was

standing wide-open with several inches of dirt acting as a brace to hold it in place.

Gabby sighed. "The back is almost as bad as the front, only with dirt instead of rain."

Wyatt grumbled under his breath. "How did the door get open?"

"Who knows. Probably an animal or something."

"Yeah, makes sense." His lips turned down, and his brow creased. "At some point this was a really nice house, but it's a wreck now. Wonder how many dust storms this place has seen."

She laughed. "By the looks of this kitchen? A lot."

Nodding, Wyatt inhaled and slowly let it out. By the sounds of it, they were both thinking it would need a lot of work.

They toured the rest of the house, and much like the kitchen, there was a layer of dirt on everything. The curtains were in shreds, and they found evidence of a nest in one of the bedroom closets. The bedroom nearest the living room was in the worst shape as the damage had spread to it because it shared a wall. The trim along that wall was warped, along with the floor. After surveying the rest of the home, they returned to the kitchen.

"So much work. It'll basically need to be gutted, an electrician called out, and then put back together."

Gabby's shoulders sagged. The dollar signs had added up to a point where she'd stopped calculating it. Even if she still had her job, there was no way she could help fix it up.

Wyatt sighed and nodded. "It would definitely need to be gutted, and that's a good call about the electrician. There's no telling what critters hid out in here or what they might have chewed on."

"These cabinets *might* be salvageable, but I don't know that anything else could be. And if that's the case, would it be worth saving them?"

"It might."

For a billionaire maybe. Sure, they'd talked about doing this when they were younger, but that was when they were kids. Not only were they ignorant about financing something like this, but they were equals at the time finance-wise. Fifty-fifty meant they contributed equally. If Wyatt was footing all the costs, it was no longer a partnership but a sole proprietorship.

Wyatt walked to the back door and stood there a second. "Let's check out the trees. From what I could see from the truck, they'll need pruning for sure."

"I had the same thought," she said, but the excitement waned with every dollar added to the project.

As they made their way to the first row of trees, he

pointed out several that looked dead. "Those will need to be replaced."

"Yeah, they've been neglected a long time. Overall, it's not too bad."

"I agree. Neglect is the issue. I think with some attention, they could be back in shape within a season or so."

Gabby smiled. "Yeah." She scanned the area. "It sure is pretty out here. I bet people would love to come here in the winter and take horse-drawn sleigh rides, drink hot cocoa, and enjoy the peace and quiet of the place."

"With the amount of work needed to fix the house, there's no reason it couldn't be turned into a bed and breakfast. People could come, check out the ranch, and have a little slice of country." The lines around his lips deepened as his smile widened. He glanced at her and winked. "The place isn't perfect, but it sure could be."

"I think so too, but…"

He turned to her, his gaze boring into her. "But what?"

She toed the ground. Should she tell him she was jobless? No, he wouldn't care. "I can't afford it even if we were being serious about starting the orchard project. I have a little in savings, but…" She motioned toward the house. "This is way more than what I've got."

"I have the money. I'm not worried about that. Bear would be thrilled for us to be a part of the ranch. That's what he's wanted all along."

Gabby held his gaze a second before shaking her head. "Wyatt, no. You may think it doesn't matter now, but what about later? What if you begin to think that I only see you as a piggy bank?"

He set his hands on his hips. "I'd never think that."

"You say that, but it only takes one little bit of doubt to ruin things. I can't. I won't." She turned to walk away, and he grabbed her by the arm. "I need to get back."

"I'm not done talking."

The conversation was over as far as she was concerned, and she was cold.

"Well, I am," she said, trying to free her arm. "I'm cold, and I want to go back to the house."

"Fine, but this isn't over." He released her and stomped to his side of the pickup. Opening the door, he said, "You coming?"

The entire West clan was so stubborn. She marched to her side and got in. "Let's go."

Wyatt started the truck and gunned it a little to get the engine heating. "So, about this orchard. We—"

"I lost my job, Wyatt." Her eyes widened as she realized what she'd blurted.

He stared at her a second. "What?"

She kept her gaze from meeting his. "I lost my job the day before I came here. I thought I was getting a promotion, but when I went to the meeting, they were letting me go. They're going a new direction, and it's out with the old and in with the new."

"I'm sorry. Why didn't you tell me before?"

She hugged herself. "I don't know. Coming back home, no job. I felt like a failure."

He was sorry. She'd spent four and a half years building a life in Charleston, only to fail. What if she went in with him and this failed too? It was only money now, but later…who knows what it'd be.

Scoffing, he said, "You aren't. You never have been. You've always put your heart and soul into everything. You always worked to be the best at whatever you set your mind to. That's why I always wanted advice from you. You always asked the questions most people didn't think to ask."

"Maybe, but maybe this is also a good thing." Gabby waved him off, frustrated that she'd let that fact slip. "And besides that, you're still bull riding. This is a lovely fantasy, but there's no way it can be a reality. It was silly talk between two teenagers."

"Yes, it can. Money isn't the only thing that makes a partnership. It's vision, determination, and hard work. Just because you don't have the money doesn't mean you can't participate. You have other things that are just as valuable."

Gabby lifted her gaze to his. "We need to get back, and there's no point in talking about this, especially since you're still bull riding."

He swore under his breath, waited a beat, and then said, "I'm not."

Her mouth dropped open. "What?"

"Well, I am, but I can't stay on eight seconds."

"Why? Because of the accident?"

He scrubbed his face with his hands and nodded. "Yes, I'm...afraid. Every time I ride, all I can think about is getting trampled. I woke up after the accident in more pain than I'd ever experienced. I panic."

Her Wyatt...frightened? No confidence? She couldn't even picture it. Was that why he'd snapped at her that first day? He was ashamed to admit he was scared of getting hurt again? Gabby had never heard him talk like this before. When she didn't say anything, he continued.

"See? I'm worthless. I've been living on ramen noodles and cheap frozen meals because I want to earn my keep. That lottery money is still just sitting in the bank, doing nothing."

She moved closer to him, laying her palm on his chest. "Oh, Wyatt, no. That's not true. You're worth more than an eight-second ride. Is that why you're wanting to fix this house up?"

He shrugged. "I thought maybe it would make me feel useful." His voice was low and thick.

She lifted her hand and palmed his cheek. "Your worth is not tied to this house, bull riding, or anything else. You have value because of your heart. You've always stood up for the little guy. When Bear wasn't around, you'd protect Bandit. Remember when Carrie Anne and I broke our arms? You're the one who hugged us and whispered that everything would be okay."

"I'm thinking I'm going to quit."

"Quit? Don't say that. You've never been a quitter in your life." She never thought she'd hear those words come from his lips. It made her ache to hear him say it.

Carrie Anne relayed that Wyatt had been hurt, but she'd never told Gabby how badly. She had figured Lori was by his side. Only, she hadn't been. He'd had his family, sure, but Gabby should have been there for him. It shouldn't have mattered how hard it would have been. He'd needed her, and she'd let him down.

He lifted his gaze to hers. "What else is there to do? If I can't stay on the bull, what's the point?"

"You keep fighting until you can."

"I know everyone thinks I'm stupid—"

"No, they don't. Wyatt, you aren't stupid."

He leveled his gaze at her. "Gabby, come on. I'm the thick-headed doofus of the family. Bear bought this place. Hunter flips houses. Josiah sells commercial real estate. And then there's me. Too dumb to really do anything with his life, so he rides bulls."

She'd never heard him talk like this before. All this time, she'd been thinking she was the only one who'd grown up while she was gone. "It takes skill to ride a bull. It's not something everyone can do. Granted, there's a two-ton animal bent on goring you to death, and that can be a little off-putting, but it does take a level of talent and courage most don't possess."

He pulled his Stetson off and set it in his lap. "I guess so," he said, but he didn't sound convinced.

She'd never seen this side of him. The one that was vulnerable and unsure. She'd always seen him as the smiling easygoing guy. Maybe she needed to treat him the same way she wanted to be treated. Not as a boulder but rather as river rocks being continually polished by the water flow.

She slipped her arms around his neck. "I'm so sorry you've been hurting."

His arms circled around her as he returned the hug, burying his face in her neck. "It's okay." He paused a few breaths before leaning back and said, "Honestly, I think I've wanted out for a while. I just haven't been willing to admit it."

"Why?"

"I want more out of life than being on the road or riding a bull." He held her gaze. "I'm starting to think I might have something better to do. Something I want more."

His lips were so close. How many times had she dreamed of him kissing her? She'd pictured moments like this where he was holding her. He'd bend down and press his lips to hers. But it was a foolish fantasy that had nothing to do with reality.

She started to pull away, but he held her. "Gabby..."

The words trailed off as he brought his lips down to hers. Warm, soft, and better than any dream or fantasy she'd ever had. He pulled back, his breath mingling with hers, and their gazes locked. It seemed as though a war was waging in him.

Just when she thought that was the only kiss she'd ever have with him, he lowered his lips to hers again. The icy air had chilled her only seconds before, but now she was on fire. It touched every inch of her skin down to her nerves.

Light kisses turned ardent and hard as the fire in her stomach raged. Her lips parted with the last brush of his lips, and he deepened the kiss as he tightened his hold on her, pressing her body into his. It was everything she'd ever wanted and more. It was her Wyatt, kissing her like he belonged to her. And, oh, how she'd wished with every fiber in her being that he'd belong to her one day.

Suddenly, he pulled back and pushed away, staring at her wide-eyed. "I'm so sorry. I shouldn't have done that. I was caught up in the moment. It's not right to do this to Bandit."

Bandit? "Wyatt…"

He held up a hand. "No. You're dating him, and I'm not that kind of guy. It was a mistake to kiss you." He gulped. "We're friends. We've always been friends—family—and that's a good place to stay."

Her breath caught with the last sentence as tears stung her eyes. Friends. There was that word again, even after sharing a kiss like that? She was the only one to feel the connection? How right it felt? She turned from him and quickly wiped her eyes. "Yeah, you're right. We've been friends a long time. No sense in messing that up."

"Exactly." He shifted the truck into drive. "We should get back to the house. It's only going to get colder out here."

Oh, she was cold. All the way to her core. So frosty it would take a direct dip in the sun to warm her. They were friends, and whatever silly fantasy she had was gone. Carrie Anne was wrong. Wyatt would never want Gabby as more.

Now, she was left to stitch up her heart again. If she could just function until Carrie Anne's wedding, maybe he'd leave for the rodeo and stay gone long enough for her to get over him. If she couldn't...she wasn't sure what she'd do.

CHAPTER 12

*H*e'd kissed her. *Kissed* her. Wyatt couldn't believe he'd made such a horrible mistake. He'd never been the kind of man to go after another man's girl. It was against every code he lived by. And he'd done it to Bandit, of all people.

The drive from the orchard to the ranch house had been quiet, tense, and awkward. As soon as the pickup had pulled to a stop, Gabby had bolted from the cab and run into the house. Instead of following her inside, Wyatt had gone to the barn to figure out why he'd kissed her. He'd never thought of her that way, but, by golly, he'd sure enjoyed it.

Everything had been fine until he'd hugged her. Whatever perfume she'd worn was a ring in a bull's nose. He'd buried his face in her neck, inhaled, and

Love Potion No. 9 had hit out of nowhere. He'd leaned back, and those dark eyes of hers were staring at him, those lips looking so soft, begging to be kissed. They'd held out a "help wanted" sign, and he'd gladly accepted the job.

What was he thinking? He'd tried to stop himself. Lord knows he'd tried. He'd thought kissing her the first time would be stale and bland because it was Gabby. Not that she wasn't wonderful, but she was his little sister's best friend, not the kissing kind. But that one kiss had blurred his vision, fritzed his brain, and the next thing he knew, he was giving eight seconds a run for, and he wasn't even on a bull.

How was he ever going to apologize to Bandit? Even the accident, as bad as it was, didn't have him this miserable.

The barn door opened, and he looked up from the upturned bucket he sat on.

Hunter closed the door and rubbed his hands together. As he approached Wyatt, he shivered and stuffed them in his coat pockets. "Man, it's cold out there. Snow's starting to come down."

"Why are you out in it, then?" Wyatt asked.

Hunter stopped a few feet away and leaned his shoulder against the wall. "Gabby ran inside, tears gushing, with Carrie Anne running after her, and I just so happened to see you slink in here. What did you do?"

Groaning, Wyatt hung his head. Did he really want to tell Hunter what had happened? That he was a lousy human being and deserved to have his lights knocked out?

Hunter let out a whistle. "It's got to be bad with the way your acting."

"I...I kissed her." He groaned. "And then told her it was a mistake."

When Hunter didn't respond, Wyatt looked up and found Hunter with his mouth hanging open.

"I didn't mean to. I know she's with Bandit. It was wrong. Horrible and wrong, and I feel awful."

Wyatt's brother looked at him, puzzled. "Wait. Bandit is dating Gabby?"

"It seems so, but that's not the issue. How am I supposed to tell Bandit what I did?"

"Did she kiss you back?"

Did she ever. For a woman dating another man, she'd given as much as Wyatt had. Her arms had tightened around his neck, and she'd pulled ever so slightly toward him, pressing her body against his. Mercy, it was a fantastic kiss.

When he didn't respond, Hunter said, "If she did, then maybe she's not dating Bandit as much as you think. Gabby's not that kind of girl. She doesn't cheat. Or, I wouldn't think so. Come to think of it, you ever remember her dating anyone?"

"No, I sure don't." In fact, Wyatt didn't remember her even talking about guys when they were younger. "Now I feel even worse. The first guy she dates, and I go and kiss her."

"Did she tell you they were dating? Like, outright?"

"Well, Carrie Anne kinda said they were, but when I asked Gabby, all she said was that they'd just started talking."

Hunter took his hat off and scratched his head. "That's it? They haven't even been on a date? A real date?"

"Not that I know of." And the way Gabby told it, it was just them talking at this point. Did Bandit even consider that dating? Wouldn't he need to ask her out on a real date for it to count?

He didn't know what he should do. Should he ask Bandit if he was dating Gabby? Or did he just let it die? Avoiding it seemed a cowardly way out, but never kissing her again? Every time the thought came to mind, Wyatt's stomach twisted.

The battle going on inside him was enough to make him want to scream, and he was going to spend the next month with Gabby. How was he going to manage that?

Wyatt's brother straightened. "Then I wouldn't sweat it. I mean, just talk to Bandit. Ask him if they're dating. Women are weird. I mean, you ever known a woman to be simple?"

Chuckling, Wyatt shook his head. "No, they're as complicated as all get-out. I've yet to figure them out."

"You're telling me," Hunter said, casting his gaze to the floor. "They can mix a man up something fierce."

Wyatt stood. "What about you? You dating anyone?"

"Nope, much to Mom's dismay." Hunter rolled his eyes.

"She's been on you about grandkids?"

Hunter grunted a laugh. "Yeah, it was my turn. Bear said she'd chewed on him the last couple of months. He was glad when she set her laser beams on me."

It was no secret that Caroline West wanted grandkids. She'd spent a few months on each of them, telling them they needed to settle down. With Carrie Anne's engagement, hopefully, it'd give them a reprieve for a while. Although, if Mom had it her way, she'd have a house full of grandchildren running around.

"I'm with Bear. After my accident, it was months

of...*when are you going to quit putting yourself in danger, settle down, and give me grandbabies?* Boy, she was on my tail about it."

Wyatt's brother looked up and smiled. "No joke. Her thing with me was, you need to at least date if you're ever going to find someone."

"Is there another reason you decided to slink into the barn too?"

Hunter straightened and rubbed his knuckles along his jawline. "Nah, I just thought I'd check on you after the scene in the house. I didn't realize you'd kissed someone else's girlfriend."

Wyatt socked him in the bicep. "Shut up. I already said I didn't mean to, and like you said, I'm not even sure they're really dating."

Rubbing his arm, Hunter eyed him. "And if they are?"

"I'll jump that ravine when I get to it. Until then, I'm keeping my lips to myself. Gabby's just a friend anyway. It was a weird moment that probably won't ever happen again."

That idea didn't sit right with Wyatt at all. Never kissing Gabby again? After that five-alarm kiss? That would take some strength Wyatt wasn't sure he possessed.

The barn door creaked open again, and their dad walked in. "Hey," he said.

"Hey," Hunter said.

"Did you just get back from riding around with Bear?" Wyatt asked.

His dad nodded. "Yeah. We were just putting up the ATVs when I saw you two slip in here. I told Amos and Bear to go on and I'd be along in a minute."

"Did you get anything figured out?"

"I think so. Bear wants to run cattle and buffalo. We've got some work cut out for us first. Can't just turn cattle out. We're going to start inspecting the fence next week. It'll give us something to do while your sister picks out dresses and all that stuff."

Wyatt stuffed his hands in his coat pockets and leaned his shoulder against the wall. "Sounds like a good start."

His dad crossed his arms over his chest. "What are you two doing out here?"

Wyatt shrugged and glanced at Hunter. "Just talking about a bunch of different things."

"Uh-huh." His dad narrowed his eyes and looked between his boys. "Like what?"

Hunter shifted uneasily. "Uh, I think I'll head back inside so you two can talk. My feet are frozen. See ya in a bit." He smirked, and as he headed for the door, a strong wind rattled the roof of the barn. "I think that storm might be here," he said, lifting his gaze to the ceiling. "Better not stay out in the barn too long." He shut the door behind him.

Figured that Hunter would bail on him.

His dad raised an eyebrow. "What's going on?"

Life? But that was a bit of a broad subject. Wyatt definitely wasn't up for another conversation about Gabby, but he was curious to know what his dad thought about Wyatt's future. "Wondering if Bear still wants someone to go in with him on the ranch. Gabby and I checked out the orchard today."

His dad's eyebrows raised. "I see. What about the rodeo?"

"I don't know." Wyatt pushed off the wall, walked to one of the stalls, and looked over the door. "Can't stay with the rodeo forever. You're the one who taught me I need to think long term. This old barn needs work, but I bet it could be turned into a real nice stable."

His dad remained quiet a little too long, so Wyatt faced him.

"What?" Wyatt asked.

"This isn't like you." He straightened and rubbed his chin. "You've loved the rodeo since the second you sat on the back of a sheep, mutton busting. You said you'd die a clown before you quit."

Wyatt scraped at a board with the tip of his boot. "I'm getting old. Aging out. It was a good dream."

"Yeah, it was." He lifted his gaze to Wyatt's, holding it a breath before adding, "That accident spooked you. Getting hurt, that wasn't easy. Not on the family, and certainly not on you."

Turning away from his dad, he scoffed. "What are you talking about? I'm not spooked. I ride just fine."

The sound of his dad chuckling made Wyatt face him again. An amused look greeted him. "You can shovel that somewhere else. What's keeping you from moving forward? Be honest."

Shrugging, Wyatt's gaze dropped to the barn floor. "I don't know. I get on the bull, and all I can think about is waking up in the hospital. I don't know what to do."

That ride constantly played in his mind. He'd wrapped his hand in the rope to hold on, the bull was perfect, and he knew he'd get a lot of points. When the gate opened, everything was going great, and not a second later, he was getting rammed against the wall. It had caught him off guard, and he'd tried to get off the bull. His hand got tangled. After that, he couldn't remember. Only waking up in the hospital, wondering if he'd ever ride again.

"Well, at least you got back on one. That's a start."

"Yeah, but, Dad, what good is it if I can't finish an eight-second ride. I'm jumping off one or two seconds early."

Closing the distance between them, his dad stopped a few inches away and placed his hands on Wyatt's shoulders. "You went through something none of us will ever understand, but I want you to know that we are all proud of you. All of us. Your momma, me, the whole family. We'll support whatever decision you make."

Wyatt's chest tightened. Proud of him for what? Becoming a loser? "Nothing to be proud of. I can't seem to get back what I had."

His dad gripped his shoulders tighter. "Son, I'm not proud of you because you win a ride on a bull or get belts or make money. I'm proud of you because of the man you've become. I'm proud of you for not quitting. Take a step back while you're here. Whatever it is that's missing, you'll find it. It might be right smack-dab in your face, and you don't even see it yet."

It was just a split-second flash, but Wyatt pictured Gabby. Their kiss. It had caught him off guard. He'd never thought of her like that before this weekend.

What kept him from even trying was the thought of their families. *If* she and Bandit stopped dating and *if* something happened between them and it didn't work out, their families could be affected. Wyatt didn't want that.

Why was it even coming to mind? It was little Gabby. But she wasn't so little anymore. She'd filled out in all the right ways, and just thinking about her made his pulse race.

He shut the thoughts down, setting an iron steak press on them. They needed to stay down this time.

"I hear ya, Dad. Maybe you're right. I'll stop thinking about the rodeo and just relax while I'm here. There's a chance I could have an epiphany and go back with my head in the game and my heart all in."

His dad dropped his hand. "That's the right attitude." He slapped him on the back. "Now, let's get inside. My earlobes are about to freeze off."

Wyatt laughed. "Yeah, now that you said it, I'm cold too."

They quickly walked to the house and stopped in the foyer to shake off the cold. "Whew, I think it's gonna snow," Wyatt said, cupping his hands to his mouth and blowing on them.

"Yeah, that's what the radar is showing too," Hunter

said, coming into view from the back of the house. "There's coffee ready if you want to warm up."

"Come have some with me and Wyatt. We're going to talk about that old barn out there. Wyatt's got some ideas."

King nodded his head toward the kitchen. "Come on. We'll hash it out, and then we'll talk to Bear and see what he thinks."

Wyatt and Hunter grinned and followed their dad. This was what Wyatt needed. Sitting at a table, talking plans with his dad. That's what had made buying the lottery tickets so fun: talking about all the ideas they had. Not the money. The last year on the road had drained him. He needed his cup filled, and being home would do that. At least, he sure hoped so.

If it didn't, he wasn't sure what he was going to do. But doing the same thing over and over again was getting old. In his mind, if he wasn't winning, he needed to hang his hat up and find somewhere else to apply his energy. Something that would make him feel accomplished and useful. Something more than eight seconds of failure.

CHAPTER 13

"Gabby?" Carrie Anne's voice came through the door. "Let me in, okay?"

What was there to talk about? Carrie Anne had been wrong. Her plan was a disaster, and Gabby's heart was in shreds. Wyatt had called kissing her a mistake. *A mistake.* Hadn't she made it clear that she'd only been talking to Bandit? That saying they were together was too strong a word? She'd sure tried.

Another knock, and Carrie Anne said, "Please? Can I come in?"

Gabby looked over her shoulder as she lay curled up on the bed with her back to the door. "Okay."

It slowly opened, and Carrie Anne stuck her head in. "What happened?" She slipped inside and shut the door behind her. "Why are you crying?"

"He kissed me."

Carrie Anne gasped. "That's great."

"And then said it was a mistake." Tears pooled in Gabby's eyes again. It was her biggest fear. That something would happen between them and then he'd call it a mistake. "That we're just friends, and he was just caught up in the moment."

The bed moved as Carrie Anne sat down and rested her hand on Gabby's arm. "I don't think he really believes that."

Gabby sat up. "How can you say that? You should have seen him. He looked...distraught. Like it was the worst mistake he'd ever made. I was the worst mistake he'd ever made. I tried..." The sentence trailed off as the words caught in her throat.

Carrie Anne pulled her into a hug and rubbed her back. "He thinks you're dating Bandit. If I know him as well as I think I do, that's why he said all that."

Pulling back, Gabby said, "But I hinted as hard as I could that Bandit and I weren't really dating. I told Wyatt that we'd only been kind of talking."

"Yeah, but Bandit is family. If Wyatt thought for a moment he was stepping in on territory he shouldn't, he'd run as fast as he could." Carrie Anne brushed Gabby's hair back. "And Lord knows I love him, but we've already established he's thick as a brick. He couldn't pick up a hint if it bit him in the butt."

"He's not stupid, and I dropped hints the size of dinosaurs."

Carrie Anne sighed. "But this is Wyatt. He's not stupid; he's just…so clueless."

Gabby grabbed a tissue from the box sitting on the nightstand and wiped her nose. "But it wasn't just a mistake. He said we were friends and that's where it should stay. He doesn't see me that way."

"Well, his lips were telling a different story." Carrie Anne chewed her lip, letting the silence stretch a moment. "Listen, I know this is hard, but stick with the plan. Give Wyatt a moment to figure out his own feelings. I'm telling you, my brother cares for you just as much as you care for him."

Oh, how Gabby wanted that. The very thought that he did care for her was dangling a carrot in front of a mule. It was all she could do not to strap that wagon on and hike the highest hill. "What if you're wrong?"

"What if I'm right?"

"I don't know, Carrie Anne. When he said we should just stay friends, it would have hurt less if he'd outright punched me."

Taking her by the shoulders, Carrie Anne locked

eyes with her. "Gabby, my brother has always sought you out. When it came to his problems, he'd find you. When he was excited and happy about something, you were the first person he'd want to tell. You've always been first. A man doesn't put a woman on the top of his list for no reason, even if he doesn't know it yet."

"But I'd do the same when it came to him. If he doesn't feel that way about me by now, then what hope is there?"

"He just needs time to put two and two together. Right now, he can't even figure out there's an equation to solve. Give him time. You've never dated anyone seriously. Never once. At no point in time have you been unavailable. You need to be unavailable so he can see what it would look like if he couldn't seek you out anymore."

That was true. Gabby had never dated anyone. Okay, yes, a date here or there, but it was never anything serious. How could it be, when all she did was compare them to Wyatt? His great smile, his dark blue eyes, the way he walked…everything. There wasn't an inch of him that didn't make her knees weak.

"Trust me on this. You've been convenient. He's never had to think about losing you. Well, now he does, and he needs to." Carrie Anne dropped her hands to her lap. "You are an amazing person. You are kind, sweet, and loveable. If Wyatt doesn't come to his senses, then you deserve better. This thing needs to end one way or another. You deserve to be loved."

Gabby lowered her gaze to the bed. As much as she wanted to disagree, she couldn't.

Even dating in Charleston hadn't been the cure for getting over him. The guys who asked her out were nice, but as much as she tried, there was never a spark. Of course, when you were still hung up on someone in another state, it was like trying to light a match underwater.

Carrie Anne took her hand. "Trust me. I'm not wrong about this."

"Okay, I'll...try." Gabby lifted her eyes to Carrie Anne. "But if he doesn't want me, then I'm done."

"You have my word. If he doesn't, it'll be his loss. He might be my brother, but if he's too dumb to see the best thing in his life is staring him in the face, then so be it."

Chuckling, Gabby nodded. "Okay."

With that, Carrie Anne smiled. "Then we stick to the plan and let him think you and Bandit are an item."

"Okay."

"Good. Let's get you cleaned up and start planning. You and Bandit are going out this week."

Gabby's eyebrows knitted together. "What?"

"You're going on a real date."

"I am? Did Bandit agree to this?"

Carrie Anne rolled her eyes. "No, something's going to come up, and he won't be able to go. Wyatt, on the other hand, will see this gorgeous knockout, ready for a night on the town, and he won't be able to resist."

Groaning, Gabby palmed her forehead. "I'm so going to regret this."

"It'll be great, and Wyatt won't know what hit him." Carrie Anne grinned. "Please tell me you brought a dress. Something that will go with those red boots of yours.

This so-called date was either going to be great or horrible. Gabby could see no way it could fall in the middle. What would happen if Wyatt did think she was unavailable for once in his life? Maybe it was time to find out.

What could it hurt to play the part? Every time Wyatt came around, she'd drop everything for him. Everything. Papers that were due, science projects... not to mention taking out the trash forever just to see his events.

Squaring her shoulders, Gabby decided it was time she stopped allowing her heart to be broken. Maybe it was time to do a little heartbreaking of her own. Maybe she could even "Achy" dance to it. With red boots.

CHAPTER 14

"**A**re you playing or sleeping with your eyes open?" Wyatt's dad asked Josiah. "I ain't got all day."

Wyatt barked a laugh. Josiah always slowed a rummy game down. Granted, he almost always won it, but it still took him forever to play. Card games were a staple between the Wests and the Fredericks. It was always tense but fun because Josiah and King were the most competitive.

As desperate as Wyatt was to keep his mind occupied, he'd have put up with anything. Kissing Gabby had messed with his head. Since their kiss, anytime she was around, it was awkward and tense—something he'd never felt between them before. Sure, they'd had arguments as all people do, but it didn't feel anything like what had been going on since that day at the orchard.

Now, anytime Wyatt got the chance to keep himself active, he took it. He'd even gone grocery shopping with his mom, which had been a horrible mistake. He loved his momma, but she'd officially turned her grandchild radar on him. When was he settling down? His answer of *I don't know* didn't work anymore. Well, it had never worked, but it worked even less these days.

"You just hold your horses," Josiah growled, breaking Wyatt from his thoughts.

Thank goodness. His older brother to the rescue. Wyatt didn't need to fall down that rabbit hole again.

Their dad leveled his eyes at Josiah. "You got nothing. Just call it and take your licks, boy."

Mrs. Fredericks laughed, bumping her shoulder against Wyatt's mom. "Those two. You think they'll ever grow out of that?"

His mom scoffed. "At this point? No."

Stephanie scooted down in her chair. "Come on, Joe, just play the game."

He glared at her. "Don't you start."

Israel set his cards down and looked at his phone. "Carrie Anne should be here in a second. Whatever she was working on, she says she's finished."

So far, the game consisted of Wyatt's parents, Hunter and Josiah, Gabby's parents and her sister, and Israel. Bear...he didn't care for card games. He was in the living room, snoozing in the recliner. Wyatt had no idea where Carrie Anne, Gabby, *or* Bandit were.

The past few days, it seemed like whatever sort of relationship Gabby had with Bandit had upped a notch. They'd almost been inseparable. For some reason, after kissing her, their being together annoyed Wyatt even more. It shouldn't have, and he tried not to be, but it didn't stop the errant thoughts that said she was with the wrong guy. Wyatt had thought about talking to Bandit, but he was going to have to accept that they were together.

He shook his head. He didn't need any of his thoughts going down that road. He needed to keep his eyes on his cards and his mind in the game. No images of Gabby or Bandit needed to mess up his concentration.

Josiah's eyes widened, and Wyatt followed his line of sight. No wonder Josiah was gawking. Gabby stood in the doorway, looking like a magazine model in a form-fitting little black dress with red boots. Her hair was hanging in loose curls flowing around her shoulders, and, man, those dark eyes of hers were sparkling like a New Year's fireworks display.

"Goodness gracious, honey, you look fantastic," Wyatt's mom said.

Mrs. Fredericks stood and walked to Gabby as Carrie Anne sidled up next to her.

Carrie Anne giggled. "She looks amazing."

Amazing? Fantastic? Did those words even do her justice? "Whoa." The word slipped from his lips before he could wrangle anything better.

Wyatt's dad twisted in his seat. "I don't think that dress is long enough."

Wyatt's mom popped his dad's arm. "Hush. It's touching her knees."

"And painted on," Wyatt said. Again, his mouth was saying things faster than his brain could work. "Where are you going in that?"

Gabby settled her gaze on him and flashed him the most dazzling smile he'd ever witnessed. "I'm going to dinner with Bandit."

"You're going out with Bandit tonight?" Stephanie dropped her cards and sat up straight.

A light pink covered her cheeks as she looked down. "Yep, he's taking me out."

Stephanie blinked a second, and her mouth opened like she was about to say something before she clamped it closed. "Are you sure you're only going to dinner?"

Wyatt jerked his attention to Gabby's sister. "What?"

"You do see how she's dressed, right?" Stephanie laughed. "That's going to be some date."

This date business with Bandit didn't sound good at all. Not when Gabby was going out looking all...dressed up.

The clutch Gabby was holding began ringing, and she fished out her phone, putting it to her ear. "Hey, I'm ready." She held up her finger and stepped away.

Carrie Anne walked to Israel, kissed him, and then sat in the chair next to him. "So, what are we playing?"

It was as if that dress was no big deal to anyone but Wyatt. It covered everything just fine, but what if some creepy guy got handsy with her? Could Bandit knock their lights out like he was supposed to? He was a good man, but he wasn't the put-your-dukes-up kind of guy. That dress called for a man with a solid right hook.

Wyatt set his cards down and stood.

"Where are you going?" asked Carrie Anne.

He might not have been the sharpest crayon, but he had enough wits to not say, *To spy on Gabby.* Instead, he used the best excuse ever invented. "Bathroom."

"Oh," his sister replied sweetly, but the look she

gave him nearly froze his boots in place. It was as if she was reading his mind and knew his real reason.

He shivered with the thought and left the table. As he reached the living room, he walked softer. His brain and his body were working in such harmony that he didn't even have to try to be sneaky. Wyatt stopped just far enough away that he could hear her clearly.

"No, it's okay. I understand." Her shoulders sagged. "I was looking forward to it. Maybe another time?"

Another time? Bandit was standing her up? What? Nothing Bandit said would make up for him ditching her.

"Sure, I'll talk to you later." She chuckled. "Okay. Bye."

She turned, and Wyatt froze. "I'm sorry. I was going to the bathroom and didn't want to interrupt you."

"It's okay." She lifted one foot and began taking off her boot.

"What are you doing?"

She stopped and shrugged. "Changing. Bandit went to town, and he lost track of time. We had reservations at the La Grande Bistro in Amarillo. No way we can make it now." Sighing, she set her clutch on a nearby side table. "It's okay. Maybe another time."

"Well…" Well, what? The last time Wyatt was alone with her, he'd kissed her. Did he risk doing that again? Especially with her looking so amazing? Man, her lips were covered in some gloss that seemed to be made of neon. It was all he could do to keep his eyes off them.

That was *his* problem, though. She looked great, and it didn't seem right for her to look that good and not get to go out. It wasn't fair that her night should get ruined just because Bandit lost track of time. She deserved a great night out. "I could take you. I mean, I'm a poor substitute for Bandit, but if you're okay with it, I'd be happy to be your plus one."

She smiled. "That's okay."

The mournful tone in her voice made Wyatt even more determined to take her out. "No, you got dressed up. There's no reason to let that go to waste. Is there a dress code for that Bistro place?"

She closed the distance between them just as Wyatt took a deep breath. Goodness, and he thought she smelled good the other day. This perfume was even better. Up close, her hair looked so soft that it took effort not to slide his fingers through it. But what really got him were her eyes. They had to be the prettiest brown eyes he'd ever seen.

He was mesmerized by her. "Geez, Gabby, you just look…"

"Too dressed up?" Her lips turned down in the corners as she glanced down.

He tipped her chin up with one finger. "No, you look stunning. There isn't a prettier woman in the state of Texas, if you ask me."

"I think you're required to say that, being family and all."

His hand dropped to his side. Family? He wasn't having family feelings at all. Right then, he could see himself taking her in his arms and kissing her. He needed to knock that off if he was taking her out. Kissing her a second time...well, there would be no excuse for that. The last thing he wanted was for things to be awkward or to betray his friend again. "That's not why I said it. Family or not, you are gorgeous."

"Are you sure you want to go out with me?"

"Absolutely." The word came all the way from his core. He wanted nothing more than to spend the evening with her. Yeah, they were family, but he didn't know nearly enough about her, and he wanted to fix that. "Am I dressed okay? All I've got are jeans and these button-ups."

Her lips quirked up. "You've always looked good to me. I think you'll be fine."

"Then I guess we should go."

Man, oh man, he couldn't remember being drawn to a woman so strongly. And if he was feeling this way already, how would he feel about her once he'd spent time with her?

He took a deep breath and tamped down the thoughts. She was Bandit's girl, and Wyatt was going to respect that. He was man enough to control himself, hopefully.

CONVERSATION on the way to the La Grand Bistro was fun and light. Whatever awkwardness that had been between them was gone, and they were back to being their old selves: teasing, joking, and talking about everything from his accident to her time at the newspaper. Overall, the two-hour drive to Amarillo was comfortable.

The restaurant lived up to its fancy name. Most of the men were in suits and ties, and there Wyatt was, sticking out like a sore thumb in his working man's attire. Gabby didn't seem to mind, though. If she did, she was doing a good job of hiding it. As for Gabby, she was not only the best dressed but the best-looking woman in the whole establishment.

Wyatt sat back and held his midsection. The meal

he'd ordered was beyond delicious and filling. "I don't think I'll be able to eat for a week."

Chuckling, Gabby nodded. "Me too, but it was so good."

"Had you been here before?" he asked, leaning forward with his arms on the table.

"No, Carrie Anne was the one who suggested it. Apparently, Israel brought her here once."

"Oh," Wyatt replied and looked around the restaurant. "Yeah, I can see Carrie Anne enjoying a place like this."

Gabby shot him a smile. "You would have preferred something a little less fancy, huh?"

He shrugged. "This is nice."

"But…" She drew out the word.

"It's stuffy. I like places where it's lively and fun. Where a couple can dance and laugh and not feel like they're interrupting other people." He could sure picture dancing with Gabby, her head back with a throaty laugh, him loving the way she felt in his arms. Maybe this was the best place to take her. He had less of a chance of getting himself into trouble.

She waited a beat, catching her bottom lip in her teeth, and then grinned. "Then let's go."

He blinked. "You'd want to go dancing?"

"Why not? These boots are comfortable, and I

don't know that I've ever been asked to go dancing. It could be fun."

No one had ever asked her to go dancing? That was a crime. Wyatt leaned forward a little more. "Gabby, would you like to go dancing?"

She giggled. "I'd love to."

He stood and pulled out his wallet, tossing down enough bills that he was positive would cover their meal and the tip. As he held his hand out to her, he said, "Then let's go."

Gabby slipped her hand into his, and it was electric. Little zaps of electricity rocketed through him and made his head swim. Had there ever been a time when a woman made him feel like this? Excited, happy, content? A bull ride didn't even compare, and not too long ago, he would have said bull riding was everything. He couldn't say that with conviction right that moment. Not when he compared it to spending time with Gabby.

Once they left the restaurant, they drove around until they spotted a place that seemed to fit what they were looking for. Inside, it sported booths and tables on the outside of a dance floor. The music was a little loud, but not too bad. Most of the people were in jeans and t-shirts. It was what Wyatt called casual and easy.

"I think I'm overdressed now." Gabby snuggled closer to Wyatt, tickling his ear as she spoke.

He shook his head. "Not hardly. You're perfect."

They found a table and sat, waiting for a song they both liked. Wyatt hoped for something slow and longer than three minutes, but he had a feeling that however long the song might be, it wouldn't be long enough.

Gabby looked around. "I'm surprised the place is so busy on a Wednesday night."

"Yeah, me too, but I guess this could be someone's Friday." He smiled.

As she brought her gaze back to his, she said, "I hadn't thought about it like that, but you have a point." The smile that stretched on her lips made him glad he was sitting down. She had to have the most incredible smile of any he'd ever seen. He couldn't remember a time when a woman had smiled his way and affected him like that.

Instead of waiting for a slow song, they went to the dance floor and joined in with the other people. Several tunes played before Wyatt got his wish for a slow song. Pulling her close as the song began, he slid his arm around her waist. How many times had he hugged her? Plenty, and none of them felt this strange.

She fit against him so perfectly, like she was personally designed for him.

"Those fast songs were fun, but I'm glad to get a little break," she said as they moved around the dance floor.

Wyatt agreed but for way different reasons. "I'll definitely need a shower before I hit the sack tonight."

She laughed. "Me too, but I've enjoyed this."

"I'm glad. I can't believe you've never been dancing. Those Charleston men don't know what's fun."

"Oh, I was too busy for dating."

He narrowed his eyes. "You didn't date?"

As she looked down, she shrugged one shoulder. "A little, but none of them went anywhere. One date here, maybe another there. I was focused on my career."

"I can see you doing that. You set your mind to something, and it's a done deal. You have determination in spades."

"Maybe. I think it's sometimes a bad thing. I don't know when to give up."

Wasn't that a good thing? Never giving up on your dream or goals? "I wouldn't think that's a bad thing."

Again, she shrugged and lifted her gaze to his. "I tend to get my heart broken. It gets tiring after a while."

Man, he hated thinking of her getting hurt. That

didn't settle well with him at all. "You could have called someone. Carrie Anne, your sister...me."

Why hadn't she called him? He'd called her a few times. Mostly just after she left, but then his career took off and time got away from him. Eventually, he didn't even think about it. Not that he didn't think about her or care about her, just...life got in the way.

"I needed to stand on my own. I'd leaned against someone my whole life."

"You can be independent and still lean on people now and then. That doesn't make you weak. I sure had to lean on people when I had my accident." It had been a humbling experience. That was a lesson he'd needed, though. He wasn't invincible, and the broken bones proved it.

She took a deep breath, seeming to consider his words. "I know, and you're right. I guess at the time, I felt like if I did, I'd never figure things out on my own."

"That stubborn streak of yours...it hasn't lessened a bit." He grinned.

Her head tipped back as she laughed. Boy, did he love the sound of it. Even more, he loved being the source of it. "Yeah, I guess it hasn't."

He spun her around and pulled her back, and she laughed again. As the song came to an end, he dipped her. Again, her head fell back as she laughed, and all he could think was that he didn't want it to stop. He straightened, bringing her with him.

The smile on her lips lit up her entire face and made her simply...breathtaking. As his gaze lingered on her lips, he leaned forward. He could kiss her. Just as a way of proving all his errant thoughts were off the mark. That he wasn't attracted to her or found himself wondering what it would be like to feel her lips on his.

Not more than a breath away, she stepped back, breaking the moment. "I guess we should, um, go sit down. Unless you want to dance to the faster songs again."

That wasn't what he wanted at all. He wanted to whisk her away, find a quiet place, and spend a few hours memorizing the softness of her skin and the taste of her lips.

Then his heart took a dive as Bandit came to mind. Her great night on the town was supposed to have been spent with another man. That Wyatt was even thinking romantic things about her wasn't right. Bandit deserved a better friend than that. Still, Wyatt couldn't shake the feeling that she didn't fit with Bandit. He'd felt that way for the past week and a half, and now, after spending the evening with her, the feeling was even stronger.

It didn't feel wrong to be with her. Everything

about the evening was right. This vivacious woman with him was exactly where she was meant to be. Did she see that? Feel it? How could she not? Their friendship was comfortable. It was easy and effortless. They...worked. They always had.

Slipping into the seat next to her, he wondered what he could do to make her see that. He didn't want to be disloyal to Bandit, but Wyatt couldn't picture himself with anyone but her. The thought hit him like a sledgehammer. Why did his epiphanies have to have such bad timing?

"Yeah," he said and cleared his throat. "Let's sit this one out and cool off a little." Most likely, that wasn't going to happen. The cooling off part. Not when she was so near.

Inwardly, he groaned. Bull riding was so much easier. It was simple. Sit, hold on for eight seconds, done. No deep thoughts. No questions. Why couldn't everything be like that?

CHAPTER 15

Tossing off the covers, Gabby sat up and swung her legs over the side of the bed. It was pitch-black outside, and she hadn't had a wink of sleep yet. She had too much on her mind. Going out with Wyatt that night had been fun and a dream come true. She could have sworn he'd almost kissed her again, but she'd stopped it. It had taken every ounce of will power to do it, but somehow she'd managed. Besides, what if he'd kissed her and then apologized again? That would have been worse.

She trudged to the door and peeked out to make sure no one was up. There was no noise floating up from the first floor, and if her family was still up, there would be. Quiet was not one of their attributes.

Once she was sure she was in the clear, she tiptoed

downstairs. As she passed the living room, she startled. "Daddy! You don't sit in a dark room at night. You'll give someone a heart attack."

He turned on a nearby lamp. "Me? How about you? You're out sneaking around. I'm older and have more risk."

She wandered over to the closest chair and turned it to face the window like her dad's. "Anything interesting out there?"

"I think I saw a few rabbits, but other than that, it's been uneventful."

"Well, we *are* out in the middle of nowhere," she said with a chuckle.

"What's got you up so late, baby girl?" He laid his head on the back of the chair.

She crossed her arms over her chest and sat back. "Oh, nothing. Just...awake."

He snorted. "You sure it ain't Wyatt West that's got your sandman in a headlock?"

Did everyone know about her crush on Wyatt West? Good thing she didn't play poker; otherwise, she'd be in the poor house. "I'm not thinking about him."

"Oh, really? That'll be a first."

"I'm over him," she lied.

Her dad lifted one bushy eyebrow and leveled his

eyes at her. "You went on a date with him last night, and now you're up and unable to sleep?"

"He was just being nice because Bandit wasn't able to take me out. I used to have a crush on him, but I've outgrown that." Now that she said it, that's exactly why Wyatt had volunteered. Which meant she'd also imagined the part where she thought he was going to kiss her. In a way, she was sad that she hadn't had the brains to figure that out sooner. It would have been a disaster if she'd actually puckered up. Talk about embarrassing.

Her dad lifted his head and looked at her. "Okay, if you say so."

She scoffed. "I have. I need to be over him. He thinks of me as a friend. I'll always be that little girl with the crush. It's foolish to hold a torch for someone who can't even see you." Wyatt had never really seen her. Ever. If he did, she sure didn't know it.

Her dad remained quiet for a moment and then said, "Talk to me, baby girl. What else is on your mind?"

Her relationship with her dad had always been like this. He was someone she could always come to. He never passed judgment or made her problems feel small. If she was going to tell anyone, it'd be him.

"I lost my job at the paper. I thought I was getting a

promotion, and they gave me a pink slip. They wanted fresh blood. Like somehow twenty-four is too old all of a sudden? I'm not seventy."

"Hey, now. I'm not too far from that, and I can tell you, fifty is the new thirty."

Gabby giggled. "Sure, Dad."

"All right, keep going. Give that boulder on your shoulder a shove."

She'd missed this too. They'd done just this thing numerous times. It was like he knew she'd need someone to talk to and was waiting for her. If she ever had kids, she wanted to have this kind of relationship with them. One where they knew they could talk to her about anything and she was never too busy for them.

"I'm thinking about getting a loan and buying the paper here in Caprock Canyon. I've been looking at the Small Business Association website. I think I can do it." She glanced at him.

He nodded. "Well, of course you can. You just need a solid plan and a good business model. We're going to need a paper once the town is prospering again."

She twisted in her chair to face him. "Exactly what I thought."

"It'll be hard work. You know a business isn't easy.

You'll be the boss, and you'll have to keep a close eye on costs."

"I know. I figure I'll look into the financials of the newspaper and see how they were fairing when they were open. If I adjust for inflation, it should give me a good idea what to expect as far as expenses and possible profit."

"Sounds like a good start."

She shrugged. "I hope so. I have some savings, and I think I'll try using the local Caprock Canyon Bank."

"That's real smart. I've known the president since she was a wee thing. They had this fella from Florida or somewhere for a while. Couldn't stand him. Iris Hastings is smart as a whip. We were glad when she came home and took the job. Haven't had a bit of trouble since she took over."

Gabby cast her gaze to the floor as she tried to remember an Iris Hastings. "Oh, yeah, I think she was a senior when I was in middle school. The high school would have them come over and talk to us. She was a cheerleader."

"Yep, her dad was a good man. Her momma is still getting around, but I heard she took a bad fall. That was one of the reasons Iris moved back. Sweet, sweet girl to do that."

It felt like the planets were coming into alignment

for Gabby. Her dad seemed to think she could pull it off. She had an in with the bank president. Okay, so maybe that was taking it a little too far, but she at least had a history with the woman. "If I'm careful, I think this could work."

"I do too. I bet Stephanie would help you with a website."

"Yeah, I thought maybe I'd ask her when the craziness of the holidays is over and I'm not on maid-of-honor duty. That also reminds me that I've got to come up with a bachelorette party. Not sure what I'm going to do yet." Especially since she hadn't even thought about it until right that second.

Her dad chuckled. "Well, it'll be nothing too wild, I hope."

Gabby rolled her eyes. "Dad, no. Carrie Anne's favorite thing is watching movies and eating junk food. I'll probably have us go to dinner at a nice restaurant. Maybe we'll go dancing or something, but that's as wild as I'll get."

"That does a dad's heart good." He smiled.

They sat in comfortable silence a while, watching as different animals made appearances. The thought of owning the orchard tugged at her thoughts a few times. It was nice being on the ranch. The quiet beauty of the land. Having miles and miles of stars to watch and partnering with someone to give families the chance to experience it themselves. It was a nice dream, but that's all it was.

"Daddy, do you really think I could pull off re-opening the paper?"

"I do, but like I said, it'll be hard work."

She nodded. "I can work hard."

Her dad stood and pulled her up with him, putting his arms around her. "Baby girl, you've got a sharp mind, a strong spirit, and a kind heart. Whatever you decide, I know you'll put your all into it. Personally, I'll just be glad to have you home, paper or not."

Until he hugged her, she didn't realize how much she'd needed her dad. It was the soothing hug that said he understood all her fears, hopes, and heartaches. That he was there for her no matter what and believed in her. "Thanks, Dad."

They stood there a moment, and then he stepped back. "It's past my bedtime. I'll see you in the morning, okay?"

Gabby's smile faltered a little. "Sure."

"What has your smile taking a dive?"

"I guess it's hard for me to have dreams without Wyatt in them. I've tried to tell myself that I'm just done, but…"

"He's been a big part of your life." Her dad inhaled

and let it out slowly. "You know, just because all the parts of a dream don't come true when you think they should doesn't mean they won't ever. I'm not saying he'll ever wise up, but don't wait. You walk on and do what you need to do to be happy."

"Yeah, you're right. And thank you."

He winked. "Go get 'em, baby girl."

She watched as he left the living room and then sat down again, the dark outside swallowing everything but a few inches out from the house. Getting her dad's approval of her idea had meant the world to her. If nothing else, it gave her the gusto to work even harder to make it a reality. He was always proud of her, but she wanted to give him an even better reason.

Maybe he was right about Wyatt too. She'd keep moving on, and if he ever decided to catch up, it would be great. If not and he was too late, then that was on him. She wasn't standing still anymore. Not for him, not for anyone. She was loving someone and setting them free, and she was going to do the same for herself.

CHAPTER 16

"Gabby?"

The sound of her name brought her back to earth. She'd spent the last week following Carrie Anne's plan and preparing for the date. Phase one was being unavailable to Wyatt. Apparently, making herself unavailable was supposed to drive him crazy. If it was working, he was doing a good job of hiding it. It did make it easier on Gabby. She wasn't stuck with Wyatt every second of the day, which was what she'd envisioned when she'd went along with the whole scheme.

Carrie Anne called her name again. "Gabby? What do you think?"

Gabby blinked and took in the dress her friend was

wearing. It was beautiful, but something was missing. "I like the lace and the empire waist, but it doesn't fit your personality."

"Where were you just now?" Carrie Anne eyed her, and the question caused everyone to stare at Gabby.

Gabby's mom patted her on the arm. "Daydreaming, huh?"

"A little. I'm sorry."

Mrs. West chuckled. "It's been a pretty long day."

"Long week," Carrie Anne added. "I'm sorry. I thought it would be easier to find my dress, but I just haven't found the right one."

Gabby's mom stood and walked to Carrie Anne. "Love, it takes time. We're happy to be here." She fussed with Carrie Anne's hair. "You're going to make a beautiful bride, and you need the perfect dress."

Stephanie took a deep breath. "Maybe we need to go to a bigger city." She looked around. "No offense to this store. I mean, I love that dress you have on, but if it isn't the one, you can't settle."

"I'd hate to do that after all their hard work. They've brought in a ton of dresses for me."

Standing, Gabby stretched her arms above her head. "Okay, then back to the drawing board. I know you had this idea of a dress, but so far, none of them have worked. How about me, Mom, Stephanie, and your mom each go pick out a dress we think will work. Something completely different?"

Carrie Anne shrugged. "Couldn't hurt. None of the empire-waist dresses have worked."

Gabby hooked a thumb over her shoulder. "Okay, you've got fifteen minutes. Pick the first dress you think will work. No empire waist." She smiled. "And…go!"

With that, Gabby spun on her heels and went all the way to the back of the store to start her search. As she looked through the dresses, she thought about her own wedding. All of her life, she'd pictured it with Wyatt. Him in a tux, her walking up the aisle, and her dad giving her away.

Over the years, her dream wedding had changed as she'd aged. At first, she'd wanted red roses everywhere. Then she'd wanted orchids because they smelled so great. The last time she'd thought about it, she'd wanted yellow roses as a symbol of their friendship.

The meal would be simple, followed by strawberry shortcake since that was their favorite. Sure, they could have a traditional cake, but nothing beat a good shortcake. Countless hours were spent perfecting the whole day.

Obviously, as she'd matured, she'd learned that

there was no such thing as perfect. Something would go wrong, but as long as Wyatt was at the front of the church waiting on her, it would be the best day ever.

"So, you're dating Bandit?" Stephanie asked.

Gabby jumped and held her stomach. "Wear a bell next time!"

Her sister laughed as she walked a couple of feet and started looking at dresses. "Answer the question."

During the last week, Gabby had made extra effort to spend as much time near Bandit as possible. Again, part of phase one of being unavailable. A few times, she'd caught Wyatt looking their direction with an unreadable expression on his face. The rest of her family mostly left her alone about it.

"Yes, I'm dating Bandit."

Her sister shot her a glance. "You've had a crush on Wyatt West since the day the earth was created. There is no way you're dating Bandit. Now, if Carrie Anne concocted a scheme to make it appear that way to make Wyatt jealous, it would make sense."

Gabby froze. "I don't know what you're talking about." The last thing she wanted was for Stephanie Can't-Keep-A-Secret Fredericks to know what she was doing.

"Please. Do I look that stupid?" She pointed a finger at her face. "That's rhetorical."

With a sigh, Gabby scooted closer to Stephanie. "Please don't tell anyone. It was Carrie Anne's idea."

"I just don't want to see you get hurt. I'll never forget how heartbroken you were that night he asked Lori to marry him. You were crushed."

Gabby chewed her lip. It was a night she couldn't forget either. "I know, and I don't want that either."

"But it's Wyatt."

Instead of answering Stephanie, Gabby looked down as she nodded. "Yeah." There was so much more she wanted to say, but she held it back. Giving it voice, speaking it, would only make it worse if Wyatt never saw her as anything more than Carrie Anne's best friend.

Stephanie took her hand. "If he's so blind that he can't figure out you're the best thing to ever come his way, it'll be on him. I don't know how this will work out, but I'm here for you if you need anything."

Gabby lifted her head and smiled. "You're not going to talk me out of it?"

"No," Stephanie said with a smile. "But I *am* going to have fun with it." She winked, spun around, and walked back to the dressing room area.

Fun with it? What did that mean? Gabby groaned and mumbled to herself, "Great. Just what I needed. More fun."

After searching through a few more dresses, Gabby picked one she thought could be a good contender. It had a ball gown skirt with a scoop neck and long sleeves made of lace. It fit the time of year, it had that princess feel to it, and it was simple. Something Gabby was pretty sure Carrie Anne could pull off.

With the dress in hand, she joined the rest of the women and gave it to the clerk helping Carrie Anne.

"Everyone is back, dear," the clerk said.

The door opened, and Carrie Anne modeled the first dress.

Stephanie grinned. "That's my pick, but the heavy wedding satin doesn't look good on you."

For a moment, Carrie Anne studied her reflection. "Yeah, I'm not comfortable in it. I like it. The full skirt is pretty, but it doesn't have the feeling of being the one."

Mrs. West nodded. "Yeah, it was a good effort, though. But, no, that's not it."

The next two dresses went much like the first. They looked okay, but they could tell by the look on Carrie Anne's face that they weren't it. Then it was Gabby's pick. She was pretty sure she'd done well when she heard a gasp come from the dressing room.

Carrie Anne stepped out, and her smile went all the way to her eyes. "It's perfect."

"It's beautiful." Stephanie looked at Gabby. "Well, you two aren't best friends for no reason."

Mrs. West joined Carrie Anne on the pedestal. "Oh, honey, it's gorgeous."

"This is it. It's comfortable. I love the sleeves. I thought the lace would be itchy, but it's so soft, and I can move my arms just fine. The skirt flows exactly how I pictured it would." Carrie Anne faced Gabby. "This is the one." Her eyes filled with tears, and her hands covered her mouth. "I'm getting married."

Her mom hugged her. "Oh, sweetheart. You're going to look stunning on your day."

Gabby smiled. It was perfect. Well, beyond perfect. It fit Carrie Anne's personality. As much as she schemed and plotted, Carrie Anne was sweet all the way to the core. She always wanted to see people happy.

"My friend is getting married." Gabby approached her. "It really is perfect."

Carrie Anne pulled her into a hug. "Thank you."

Patting her on the back, Gabby took a deep breath. "I'm so happy for you."

They released each other as the clerk approached. "Now for the real work. Let's get this dress fitting like a glove for your big day."

Gabby went back to her chair and sat down. Her

mom sat in the chair beside her, leaving the clerk and Carrie Anne's mom to talk fitting details.

"That's going to be you one day." Her mom patted her hand.

"Maybe."

Her mom waved her off. "Oh, don't give me that. There's a young man out there who will come along, know he's got one of the best girls on earth, and never let you go. He may not even be that far away."

"What?" Gabby swallowed hard.

"You heard me."

Did her mom know too? Geez, did she have a sign up or something?

"Of course I mean Bandit." Her mom gave her a smile and a side-eye. It was the kind that said, *If you buy that, I've got beachfront property in Arizona for sale.* Then she winked. Great. With that, her mom stood and joined Mrs. West.

Gabby dropped her head against the back of the chair, squeezed her eyes closed, and sent up a silent prayer that...well, she didn't know what to hope for. That had always been her problem. Hoping and then having the rug pulled from under her. Maybe what she needed most was the ability to accept *no* as an answer and then move on. Perhaps that's what she needed to be hoping for. The ability to let it go. Better yet, to let Wyatt go.

lancing to his right, Wyatt tried to think of something to say to Gabby as they drove to Lubbock for the day. That hadn't been the plan when they'd woken up, but Carrie Anne had mixed up her times, booking both her cake tasting in Lubbock and her final dress fitting appointment in Amarillo at the same time.

At first, Bandit was supposed to go with her to Lubbock, but something had come up, and he couldn't. So, at the last minute, Carrie Anne had asked Wyatt so she didn't have to go alone. With only a couple of weeks left and Christmas falling right in the middle of that, there was no time to reschedule things. Plus, as Carrie Anne had pointed out, Gabby was her best friend. If anyone could pick a cake flavor, it would be her.

Wyatt didn't mind taking her, but ever since their...date, he'd felt a little weird around her. That feeling grew every time Wyatt saw her with Bandit over the past week. The two of them just didn't fit together, and Wyatt couldn't decide if that was because he really believed it or because Carrie Anne's little speech was getting to him.

He turned his attention back to the road and tried to think of a topic that would be easy to discuss. Something that would make the weird feelings go away so she could get back to being family, the kind he didn't want to hold and kiss. "Uh, you excited to taste cake?" It was lame, but it was all he could think of at the moment.

She shrugged. "I guess. I mean, it's cake. How bad could it be? Her favorite thing is chocolate, so I suspect if it's good, that'll be the flavor to pick."

"True." He chuckled. If anything, his baby sister was rather predictable. "Have you ever wondered about your wedding? I have. Sort of. I'd want something simple." Great. What line of questioning was this? Wedding equals a couple. Couple equals kissing. He was trying to put that out of his mind, not make it all he could think about.

She kept her gaze out the side window. "Yeah, I always pictured it in the spring. When it's not too hot or cold. I've always thought an outdoor wedding would be nice. Yellow roses, family and friends, and strawberry shortcake."

Shortcake? That was his favorite cake in the world. Well, it was both of theirs, but he'd never envisioned it to be the cake served at his wedding. Not that he'd spent a lot of time thinking about it, but now that she'd brought it up, it was perfect. "Why am I not surprised about the cake?"

"I think if you're going to have a cake, it may as well be something that you enjoy. It may not be the most traditional, but it sure would be tasty."

"I have to agree with you there."

She turned her head to look at him. "Have you ever thought about your wedding? I mean, when you proposed to Lori, I suspect you guys talked about it a little."

One of his worst mistakes. He couldn't even remember why he'd done it. He'd brought Lori home to introduce her to their families at one of their family dinners, he'd heard Gabby talking about moving to Charleston, and the next thing he remembered was proposing to Lori. It had been so strange. To this day, he had no idea why he'd done it.

"Not really. It didn't last very long."

Gabby twisted in her seat. "Why? I mean, I know you guys were off and on, but I figured that would be over once you asked her to marry you."

"I did too, but…" He tightened his grip on the steering wheel. "She cheated on me."

"What?"

Glancing at Gabby, he nodded. "Yep, I was on tour with the rodeo. I came back as a surprise for her birthday and caught her on a date with someone she worked with. There was no more on and off for me. It was just over."

"I can't believe she did that." She leaned across the cab and placed her hand on his arm. "I'm sorry."

He covered her hand with his. "Things happen for a reason, but thank you."

"That's true." Wyatt half expected her to pull her hand away, but she didn't. "I'm just sorry you had to go through that."

"Me too, but the thing I had with Lori had to stop. I don't even know why I let it go on as long as I did. We weren't right for each other. We didn't want the same things."

"Like what?" This time, Gabby did pull her hand away, and Wyatt hated it. Twice now, she'd offered comfort, and both times, he'd felt an emptiness when she moved away.

Resisting the urge to pull her close, Wyatt said, "She wanted to move to a big city, and I didn't. She didn't want children." He glanced at Gabby. "And I did. She wanted all these grand things when what I wanted was the simple stuff."

Gabby smiled. "She didn't want to run an orchard or anything like that."

"She especially didn't want to do that. You should have seen her face when I told her about it. There was no way that was happening." He chewed the inside of his cheek. "What's really sad is that after I found out she was cheating, I was relieved."

"I never understood why you kept getting back together with her."

"I don't have a good reason." He sure wished he did. How many times did they break up? Each time, he promised himself there wouldn't be a next time, and Lori would find a way to change his mind. "In a way, I think I was glad she cheated. No matter what she said or how much she tried, after that, I was officially done."

"I guess it was better to find out before you married her than after."

With a chuckle, he nodded. "Boy, ain't that the truth. I can't even picture being married to her." He shivered with the thought. "I think I would have been miserable."

Gabby laughed with him. "Then it's a really good thing you didn't marry her."

"I feel like that accident made me grow up. Until then, I'd always seen myself as a kid. I loved riding bulls. It was fun, and that's all I wanted. After, I had a lot of time to think. I want more than fun; I want purpose." That was the first time he'd said it out loud. Before this conversation, he didn't have the words. He just had feelings he couldn't explain.

Being with Gabby always loosened his tongue and made his brain work. She'd always had that effect on him. That was the reason he always went to her. She made him...function better. What would it be like if Wyatt no longer had her? If she got serious with Bandit, everything would change. Just the thought made his chest constrict.

The last five years had been a taste of what it would be like to not have her in his life. He didn't like that at all, especially now that he realized his life was empty without her. If she married someone, there'd be no more Wyatt and Gabby. He'd have to let her go completely. How was he supposed to do that?

She nodded. "I guess it would make you think, but you can have purpose doing what you love."

Wyatt shrugged. "I guess. Hadn't thought about it like that."

"I think sometimes we have this idea of what purpose looks like. It's so entrenched in us that we can't see another way. Most often, a big event pulls us out and makes us reevaluate things." She sighed.

Glancing at her, he asked, "How about you?"

"What? A big event?"

"No, well, I guess it could be a big event, depending on what happened. But did you ever get serious with anyone?" For some unknown reason, he was especially interested in the answer.

She shook her head. "No, I was too busy. First with college and interning at the paper, and then once I graduated, I was still busy. I kinda threw myself into my work."

"I know you said you didn't date, but I really find that hard to believe."

Shrugging she said, "Well, believe it. I tried, but most of the time it was just dinner, and there never was a spark. What was the point in prolonging the inevitable? I wasn't interested."

"Have you ever been interested in anyone, besides Bandit, that is?"

Minute after minute ticked by as the silence in the cab grew until it was so thick he could touch it. What was taking her so long to answer? And why did it bother him that it was taking this long?

Finally, she nodded. "Yeah, there's been one, but it didn't work out."

He should have felt bad for her, but instead, he felt relieved. It made him feel like a terrible person. Being glad she was miserable wasn't right at all. "I'm sorry."

"It's okay." She fidgeted with the hem of her shirt.

"I think if something's meant to be, though, it'll happen." Hopefully, she wasn't meant to be with Bandit. The second it flitted through his mind, he felt like a jerk. Bandit was his friend, and so was Gabby. He wanted them both to be happy...just not with each other.

"That's true." Her voice was so soft that he barely heard her.

Reaching across the seat, he covered her hand with his. "Gabby, you are a beautiful woman. Smart, funny, easy to talk to. Kind and generous to a fault. If that guy can't see what he's missing, he's an idiot."

The second it was out of his mouth, he nearly choked on his own words. Had Carrie Anne been right about Gabby having feelings for him? Had he just come out and asked? Nearly kissing her must have really messed with his head. Inwardly, he groaned. Why had his sister said anything? Everything was going great until she'd done that. He just needed to remember Gabby was family, and more than likely, she was talking about a guy in Charleston or something. The subject needed to go in a different direction before he did something stupid.

Maybe he could convince her to stay in Caprock Canyon. If that guy was in South Carolina, getting her away from him might help her. Plus, the town would need a newspaper, and it would get bigger as more people moved back to town. "Are you still going back to Charleston after the wedding?"

Her eyebrows drew together as she took a deep breath. "I don't know. Part of me thinks it's good for me to be out there and on my own. The other part has missed my home. It would be fun to maybe see about getting that newspaper running again. I do have a little savings. Not open-an-orchard kind of money, but maybe I could get a loan for the rest."

He scoffed. "You don't need a loan. I've got plenty. More than plenty. If you want that paper, it's yours."

"No, that's not...I need to do it on my own."

Wyatt scowled. "I don't understand. We win this

money, and no one wants it. What can one person do with a billion dollars? What's the point in having it if all the things you want to do involve people who refuse to take it?"

She braced her hand against the seat and leaned over. "Wyatt, it's not that people don't want to take it. It's that...we want to be able to say we did it. It's not the same if someone just purchases something. How will a person know it's a success if there's no chance for failure?"

"Why does there need to be a chance for failure when there doesn't have to be? What if you have the money to just do something because you love it?"

"Because...there's also the issue of not wanting to come across as using the people we love...or care about." She straightened as she cleared her throat. "I mean, our families are close. No amount of money is worth ruining our relationships."

Wyatt shook his head. "I know, but that only means I want to share it even more. I want to share my good fortune with the people who mean the most to me. Gabby, you're one of my closest friends. I want to share my good fortune with you. And we're family."

Crossing her arms over her chest, her lips pinched together. "I appreciate that, but that's not a good idea."

She twisted a little in the seat until her back was nearly to him.

He placed his hand on her shoulder, and she shrugged it off. "Are you okay?"

She sniffed. "I'm getting a headache."

"We've only got a few more miles to Lubbock. I can stop to get you something for the headache and a drink."

"Thank you," she said softly. "I appreciate that."

From that point, Gabby didn't speak another word to him. He wasn't sure what had happened, but something in his gut said it was more than a headache. The feeling grew when he caught her wiping her eyes a few times. Was she crying? If she was, why?

He pulled into a gas station on the outskirts of town and parked. As she went to get out of the pickup, he caught her hand. "Gabby, did I do something to hurt you? If I did, I didn't mean to. On my honor, I promise I didn't."

She shot him a glance over her shoulder. "No, you're fine. It's...it's just this headache." With that, she pulled free, and it looked to Wyatt like she nearly ran to the bathroom inside the station.

Why didn't he believe that? They didn't keep secrets from one another, or at least they hadn't until now. What had he said that could have upset her?

Offering to buy the paper so she could stay in Caprock Canyon wasn't for her; it was for him. It kept her close. In between rodeo events, he could come home, and she'd be there. He kinda liked the idea of seeing her in between events. It was for purely selfish reasons. Maybe if he explained it like that, she'd understand.

Besides, if she and Bandit were serious, wouldn't she want to come home? This worked out for all of them. She got to be home with Bandit, and Wyatt got...nothing. If her relationship with Bandit was serious, even if she was close, she'd be with Bandit and not spending time with him.

The idea of her being with Bandit bugged him worse than a thousand flies at a picnic. He lightly punched the steering wheel. What was wrong with him lately? It was like he was looking for his glasses while they were right on top of his head. He let out a frustrated sigh. It seemed, as of late, he just couldn't think straight.

How was he going to fare when Gabby could no longer be the person he turned to? If problem-solving was hard now, it would be even harder without her. It sure had been this past five years without her.

Maybe he'd just buy the paper and surprise her. He'd talk to Carrie Anne and come up with a plan to keep Gabby home. If anyone could scheme, it was his sister. She and Gabby were best friends too, so there was a chance she'd be just as desperate as he was. At least he had the start of an idea. When he got back home, he'd work out the details with his sister. Together, they'd figure out something.

CHAPTER 18

The pretend headache Gabby suffered from earlier was no longer fake. Holding back her tears as best as she could had caused a tension headache. After getting a drink at the gas station, they'd continued on to the bakery. She'd purchased some aspirin and taken it, but if anything, her head hurt worse. That's what she got for lying. Wyatt had been sweet, apologizing for whatever he'd done to hurt her. She should have been used to being called family at this point, but he'd said it, and it had been an arrow to the heart.

It wasn't just how he saw her. Him wanting to buy the paper was a sweet gesture, but that's not what she wanted. Taking money from him would only make it worse. Every time she walked into the newspaper office, she'd think of him. And if this plan of Carrie Anne's didn't work, how could she ever really move on if all she ever did was think of Wyatt?

Closing her eyes, Gabby cleared her thoughts. This wasn't the time to think about all of that. She had a job to do for Carrie Anne, and that meant sitting in a bakery, tasting cake, and hoping the headache would dissipate soon.

None of the cake tasted great, and Gabby was sure it wasn't the cake's fault. The headache was making it hard to like anything.

"This lemon is sure good," Wyatt said as he finished the bite. "Man, all of it is good."

So far, they'd tried half a dozen flavors, and with every sample, the headache slowly worsened, making her stomach turn. It made her glad they'd started with the chocolate. It had been all right, which probably meant it would've been fantastic if she didn't feel so bad.

The woman, Jasmine Green, owner of This Takes the Cake, smiled. "Thank you."

It was a cute place. Large display cases were filled with fresh offerings of cupcakes, cake pops, whole cakes to go, cookies, and truffles. Of course, there were also offerings of drinks for those looking to make use of the dozen or so tables and chairs. The decorations were cute with little signs and sayings written on the walls. Normally, Gabby would have been excited to try such a place.

She took a small bite of the pistachio and tried to think about the flavor. "Yeah, I think they're all good."

"That strawberry was the best, I think." Wyatt cut another piece off the sample. "This is what I'd want, but it's not my wedding."

"She wanted three tiers, is that correct?" Jasmine asked. She was maybe in her late twenties, early thirties.

"Yes, three," Gabby replied. "And the groom's cake."

They tried a few more flavors ranging from red velvet to spice. If her head didn't hurt so badly, she'd actually enjoy trying all the flavors. They were incredibly moist with intense flavor. The different flavored fillings weren't overly sweet. In all, if Gabby were to get married, she'd most likely want to use the same bakery as Carrie Anne.

Wyatt's gaze roamed the table. "But how do we choose?"

Rubbing her temple, Gabby tried to concentrate on the actual wedding cake and picture it in her mind. She knew Carrie Anne well enough that she'd want mostly chocolate. "Israel's favorite flavor is red velvet, so we'll go with that for his," Gabby said. "And for the wedding cake, how about this: the first layer will be chocolate with vanilla icing, and the second will be another chocolate one with white raspberry frosting. This way she has her white wedding cake and also the chocolate she loves."

Wyatt grinned. "Those both sound good to me. What about the third layer? We could do strawberry for that one."

"That would be for us."

"We did drive several hours to test cake. I think that should be worth one layer of cake," Wyatt teased.

Gabby lightly slapped him on the arm. "No, but can you do a lemon cake with coconut and pineapple frosting? Like a piña colada cake? She loves those. Well, the virgin ones."

"Actually, we can," the baker replied. "We've done a couple of those."

"Then that'll be a good surprise for her." Gabby rubbed her temple and winced. The headache was moving from the back of her head and settling behind her eyes.

While Jasmine scribbled down the cake flavors, Wyatt leaned over. "You okay?"

"It's just this headache."

"Is it a migraine?"

She shrugged. "I don't know. Maybe?"

Without looking up from her clipboard, the baker read the notes back for confirmation.

"Right," Gabby said.

"Okay," the baker said, again writing on her notepad. "And when she called, she said the cake would need to be delivered by two in the afternoon on New Year's Eve. Is that still correct?"

Wyatt nodded. "Yep, that's still the plan."

"Okay, we'll get working on this." Smiling, she shook Gabby's hand and then Wyatt's. "See you on New Year's Eve."

Gabby stood, picking up her purse and shouldering it. "Thank you."

"Yes, thank you," Wyatt said and stood. "This was great."

They walked to the door, and his hand came to rest on the small of Gabby's back. "Have you got anything for your headache?" he asked.

The bell ringing above the door may as well have been a gong. "I've got some motion sickness stuff. I think I'm going to take that. It usually makes me drowsy. Maybe a little nap will help."

He kept his hand on her back, guiding her to the truck and then helping her get in. "Do you want me to get you something else to drink?"

"No, it probably doesn't taste great now that all the

ice is melted, but the drink from earlier should be fine."

"You sure?" he asked, cupping her cheek. "I'll get you whatever you need."

This was the exact reason she loved him. He was always tender, sweet, and caring. He did it without even thinking about it. "I'm sure."

He leaned in and kissed her forehead. "Okay. But if anything changes, you tell me."

"I will."

Giving her one last look, he paused and then shut the door before jogging around the front and getting in. He started the truck just as she'd finished fishing her medicine out of her purse. She tossed them back with a long draw of her drink and hoped they'd kick in sooner rather than later. Laying her head back, she closed her eyes and hoped she'd feel better by the time they got home.

CHAPTER 19

*I*t had been about an hour since Gabby had fallen asleep. She'd just started to doze when Wyatt convinced her to lie down and use his leg as a pillow. At the time, he thought he was just being practical, but now he realized he'd just wanted her closer.

Just as he glanced down, she mumbled something in her sleep and draped her arm across his lap. He slid his fingers through her silky soft hair, pushing it back from her face. Something he wouldn't be able to do if her relationship with Bandit got serious, or more serious.

The idea bothered Wyatt. He couldn't be the only one who felt Bandit wasn't right for Gabby. Although, it didn't seem to bother her. She hung all over him.

Anytime Wyatt saw them together, it was always her making the move. At times, it almost felt as though Bandit was an unwilling participant, which didn't sit right with Wyatt. Either a man wanted a woman or he didn't. You didn't string someone along. It wasn't honorable to do that.

Of course, the same could be said for him and his relationship with Lori. But that wasn't him doing the leaving and coming back. It was always Lori dumping him and then coming back. He was still angry with himself that he'd done that so many times. It shouldn't have taken her cheating on him to realize he didn't want to be with her.

At least it had ended, but he'd grown increasingly lonely. Maybe that was why he'd taken her back each time. He'd hated being all alone, and at the time, it was better to have a warm body than an empty space.

"What's got you thinking so deeply?" Gabby asked.

Wyatt jumped a little, and the truck slightly swerved. "Gracious, woman. Give a man a heart attack!"

She sat up and giggled. "I'm sorry. I didn't mean to scare you."

"I'm not scared. Just surprised."

"Right."

He glanced at her and rolled his eyes. "Are you feeling better?"

She yawned and stretched. "Yeah, the headache is gone."

"You look like you're still tired."

"I am, but," she said, rolling her head, "I think I woke up because my neck was hurting."

Wyatt slid his arm around her waist and pulled her flush against his side. "How about resting your head on my shoulder?"

"You don't have to do that."

He kissed her forehead. "I don't mind at all." And he didn't mind how great it felt to have her tight against him.

Her nose brushed against his neck as she laid her head down. "I really like this cologne you wear." She took a deep breath. "I always have, but I think I told you that a long time ago."

"I remember." He blinked.

Holy smokes.

That's why he wore it. Now the full memory of the day rushed back with motion-picture quality. He'd been playing football with Bear, and Gabby had come over to meet Carrie Anne before their dates took them to their senior prom. She'd said hello, and he'd done a double-take. Man, she'd been a treat for the eyes.

The dress had been perfect on her, and of course, it had been red. It hugged her curves so well, like a neon sign screaming, *Look at me*. Wyatt's concentration on the game had faltered, and he'd taken a ball to the gut. It had laid him out. Next thing he knew, she was hovering over him, asking if he was all right.

He could remember just nodding because he was speechless. The sun had hit her just perfectly, haloing behind her. For a moment, he thought he was looking at an angel. Finally, he'd mustered enough wits and told her she was beautiful. She'd smiled and kissed his cheek before thanking him for the compliment.

Then she'd said she liked his cologne. From that point on, he'd worn it anytime he knew she'd be around. He hadn't even realized it until now. For just a brief second that year, he'd wondered what it would be like to ask her out. It had been quick, but that peck on the cheek had affected him more than he'd been willing to admit.

The whole thing had shaken him up. His thoughts had run rampant with pictures of Gabby and him together. But she was like his sister, and there was no way he could go there, so he'd shut those thoughts out before they'd had a chance to take root. He'd told himself that if a relationship with Gabby went sour, it could affect their whole family. He'd pushed the

THE BEST FRIEND'S BILLIONAIRE BROTHER

thoughts so far down that he was only now remembering them. How would their lives have turned out if he hadn't rejected those thoughts back then?

She brushed her nose across his skin again as she got comfortable, and goosebumps raced down his arms. "I've missed home."

"I've missed you." He kissed the top of her head and shocked himself. He was sure she didn't hear it, though, as soon as she breathed out. The way her body relaxed against him said she was asleep again. He tightened his arm around her, enjoying the feel of her next to him. Boy, did she fit. He had missed her. Missed her smile and her laughter and her—all of her.

Again, the thought of what would happen to the family if they dated and something went wrong flitted through his mind. At the same time, he couldn't help but wonder what it would be like if things did work. Having someone by his side, wanting the same things he did, and coming home to her smile each day.

It wasn't that Bandit wasn't right for her; it was that Wyatt couldn't let him be. It was why Wyatt's relationship with Lori never went anywhere. Because somewhere down deep, his soul was screaming that he needed Gabby. He was just too clueless to hear it.

Wyatt's heart raced as things began to make sense. All the times he'd leaned on her wasn't because she was his little sister's best friend. It was because she was his other half. Moments that Gabby leaned on him made him happy because he loved being needed by her. Since she'd been gone, he'd been miserable, and it had just hit him why.

He cared for her…maybe more than cared for her.

Carrie Anne's words were like bricks being set on top of his chest. *One of these days, you're going to figure out the real answer to that question, and she'll have moved on. You're going to wake up one day and realize you've lost her.*

And she was in a relationship with Bandit. She'd moved on, and here Wyatt was, regretting that it had taken too long for him to realize exactly what she meant to him. If he said anything now, it would be a jerk move. As much as he cared about Gabby, Wyatt cared about Bandit too.

Even if Bandit didn't seem as into Gabby as Wyatt thought he should, that didn't mean it gave Wyatt permission to try to steal his girlfriend. Maybe the guy was just shy and didn't like public displays of affection. What if the guy just liked his privacy, and it had nothing to do with how he felt about Gabby?

It was a conundrum for Wyatt. Did he approach Bandit and ask the man if he was serious about Gabby? It was possible they were very serious. They'd known each other a long time. Thinking about it made Wyatt feel disgusting. Barging in on someone's relationship just because a light bulb had finally gone off didn't seem right to him. That was Wyatt's fault for not taking his chance when he had it.

He set his cheek against Gabby's forehead, and his heart ached at the thought of not being with her. But he wanted her happy more than anything. If Gabby had moved on, Wyatt would just have to accept it. If he really cared about her, he wouldn't want to mess up her relationship.

Shaking his head, he grumbled to himself. All these weird thoughts and feelings were Carrie Anne's fault. Planting that suggestion that Gabby had feelings for him had weaseled their way into his subconscious, and now he was all out of sorts. When he got back to the ranch, he was talking to his sister and straightening this whole thing out. She was the one who started the whole thing, and she'd be the one to fix it.

THE ENTIRE DRIVE HOME, Wyatt's thoughts had gone in circles. By the time he parked the truck, if someone had asked him which way was up, he couldn't be certain he'd point the right direction. There wasn't an inch of him that wasn't at war.

It didn't help that Gabby was beside him, arm around his neck and breath tickling his skin. She was warm and perfect, and the longer he held her, the more he didn't want to let go, which was why he was still sitting in his parked truck ten minutes later, debating whether he should carry her to her room or continue watching her sleep. Either option kept her in his arms a little longer.

Before he could think too much about it, she stirred, and he took it as a sign that he should wake her up.

"Hey," he said. "We're home."

Taking a deep breath, she opened her eyes and lifted her head. "Wow, I can't believe I slept the whole way." She dropped her arm from around his neck and covered her mouth as she yawned. "I didn't mean to do that. I just wanted the headache gone."

"Is it gone?"

"Yeah."

"Then I guess you slept the right amount." He studied her face as the last little bit of light streamed in through the windows. She was so beautiful...and kiss-able. Is this what it would be like to wake up next to her? He'd never thought about that before, but now that he was, he sure liked the idea.

With a chuckle, she lowered her gaze. "I guess so. I bet your arm is numb from me sleeping on you."

As she started to put space between them, he tightened his hold on her. The involuntary response took him off guard, but at the same time, he wasn't ready to let her go. "My arm is fine. I'm just glad you're feeling better."

"I am. Thank you. I'm sorry I wasn't more fun."

Wyatt tipped her chin up with one finger, and whatever he was about to say was lost on its way from his brain to his mouth. Her lips were so close and full and perfect. The most kissable lips of any woman he'd ever known. It'd been a huge mistake last time, and nothing about her relationship status had changed. She was in a relationship, and nothing about that had changed on the drive back from Lubbock.

To keep himself out of trouble, he pressed a kiss to the side of her face and whispered, "I had fun because I was with you." He'd thought it would help, but the second his lips touched her skin, he was in trouble.

He skimmed his fingers along her jaw as his lips parted, leaving feathery kisses all the way to her lips. They were just as incredibly soft as the last time. His hand cupped the back of her neck, and he brushed his lips across hers. The cab of the pickup was so quiet that he could hear her breath catch when he caught her top lip in his teeth, coaxing her lips open.

A soft moan came from her as he deepened the kiss, and her arms circled his neck. He moved from her lips, leaving a trail of light kisses along her jaw. Her head fell back, allowing him to taste her delicate skin. Again, she moaned, and he trailed kisses back to her parted lips.

There had never been another time he'd felt like this. Kissing her was magical. Better than magical. Better than riding a bull, a cheering crowd, or winning buckles. It was perfect.

He left her lips again, pressing kisses from one cheek to the other. "Gabby…"

With the whisper of her name, she pulled back and held his gaze. "I'm so sorry. I shouldn't have done that. I need to go."

He panicked. "No, this was my fault. I'm sorry. We're family, and I guess…Well, I don't have a good excuse."

Gabby opened her door, and it looked like she was going to say something then thought better of it. "Yeah." She moved to jump out, but he grabbed her hand.

"Wait." He couldn't just come right out and say

what he was thinking. If she was single, it would be a different story, but she wasn't. There was nothing simple about this whole situation. "What if I quit the rodeo? I'd stay here. You could stay and run the paper. We could...fix up the orchard together." Surely she'd understand what was he was trying to say. He wanted to figure out what this was because no matter what he tried to tell himself, this was more than friendship. "I could settle down."

"Settle down?"

"Well, yeah, I mean, you'd be here, and we've got this opportunity to fulfill a dream." Only his dream had broadened in the last few weeks to include her.

For a breath, she just stared at Wyatt. "Why *did* you kiss me?"

If he said because he wanted to, it would make him sound like a horrible person. "I don't know. You were there, looking up at me, and..." He raked his hand through his hair.

She blinked a few times. "That's it?"

"Yes, I mean, no. That's—" How did he say what he felt without coming across as selfish? "We're friends. Good friends...and you're with Bandit."

She yanked her hand away. "That's all I'll ever be to you, isn't it? Carrie Anne's best friend. Your friend. Family. Nothing more."

Geez, he was messing this whole thing up. "You are those things, but—"

Gabby held up her hands, cutting him off. "I'm done. I can't do this anymore."

Before he could make a move, she was out of the truck and in the house. He'd never seen her move so fast. His heart hammered against his ribs as he tried to make sense of what had happened.

Yes, she was his friend and she was family, but she was more than that. Only, it wasn't so simple as just stating it. Not until he had a chance to come up with a way to approach Bandit about it. It was bad enough that he'd already kissed her—twice—but to butt in without even having a conversation with the man she was dating?

He scrubbed his face with his hands. What a gigantic mess he'd made, and all because he was being selfish and self-centered. He wasn't the center of the universe, but he'd sure behaved like it. Taking liberties that he had no business taking.

Not only was he lying to her, but he was lying to himself. He'd kissed her because he wanted to kiss her. Ever since their first kiss, that's all he'd been thinking about, and when the chance presented itself, he'd taken it. Not only that, but it was an incredible kiss.

A kiss that he'd stolen...again. She was dating

Bandit, and Wyatt had done the one thing he'd promised himself he'd never do. What kind of man was he? He wanted to blame Carrie Anne, but if he was honest, he knew it wasn't her. It was him.

Since the moment he saw Gabby at the airport, something had shifted in him. The only thing Carrie Anne's little speech had managed to do was give those thoughts words. No matter how much he tried to tell himself that Gabby was only family, she wasn't. She was more than that, and he knew it.

He sucked in a lungful of air and let it out slowly. His excuse for not pursuing Gabby in the past was that he didn't want to hurt their families, but the reality was, he was scared. He'd been fearless with Lori because he knew it would go nowhere.

With Gabby, the opposite was true. It had the potential to last. The real fear was that he'd mess it up. Maybe it was time to man up and face those fears, but first, he needed to figure out what he needed to do next. At the moment, he had no idea which way to go.

CHAPTER 20

Stepping back, Gabby looked over the decorations for Carrie Anne's bachelorette party. She'd decided it was probably best to have it before Christmas because afterward, there would be a frenzy of activity leading up to Carrie Anne's wedding.

She'd thrown herself into planning the party to keep her mind off Wyatt. It was her own fault for allowing the kiss to happen. He'd already been cheated on, and he thought she was dating Bandit. The last thing she wanted Wyatt thinking was that she was anything like Lori. But for him to *still* think of her as a friend...she couldn't do it any longer.

Of course, that didn't make the fact that he called it a mistake hurt any less. It was absolutely irrational since she had said it first, but Gabby had learned when it came to Wyatt, there was nothing rational about her. Giving herself something to do had helped, though, and she'd worked to avoid him the last few days.

"Stop fussing with it," Gabby's mom said. "It looks fine."

"People are going to start arriving in about an hour. I just want everything to be perfect for Carrie Anne."

Instead of a restaurant, Gabby had opted for Bear's home. Of course, she'd okayed it with him first and then asked if Bandit would mind cooking for them. Nothing big or fancy, just some finger sandwiches and punch.

Stephanie stopped between Gabby and their mom. "No, I think Gabby is right." She stepped forward and messed with the candy centerpiece. "There. That looks good to me."

Gabby nodded. "Yes, now it is. Thanks."

Her mom touched her arm. "You should probably get changed. Stephanie and I will finish the rest, okay?"

With a chuckle, Gabby looked down at her clothing and touched her hair. "Yeah, guess I built up a sweat, huh?"

"I could smell you from my room," her sister teased.

Gabby playfully popped her arm. "Shut up. I'm gonna go now."

She left the room, walked through the house, and hit the stairs at a jog. As her feet touched the top of the landing, she bounced off a body, smacking her head hard against the wall. She sucked in a sharp breath, her vision blurring.

Strong arms grabbed her around the waist. "Whoa, Gabby, are you okay?" Wyatt asked.

She wanted to respond, but she was dazed. Her knees buckled, and a second later, she was being lifted into his arms. The next thing she knew, she was being lowered onto a bed.

Wyatt sat next to her. "Gabby, are you okay?"

"I...I think so." She blinked a few times to clear her head.

"I'm so sorry. I was rushing to get downstairs and not paying attention."

She lifted onto her elbow and said, "It's okay. I think I'm all right now."

He took her jaw in his hands, his eyes roaming over her face. "Are you sure? You nearly passed out." He dropped his hands from her face but continued to keep his intense gaze on her.

"Guess I'm not just tenderhearted; I'm tender-headed too." She chucked and winced. "I may need some aspirin." She pushed herself into a sitting position.

Wyatt took her in his arms and held her. "You scared the dickens out of me." He pulled back just a fraction, kissed the side of her face, and held her tight again.

"It's okay, Wyatt. It was just an accident. I wasn't watching where I was going either." Now that her head was clearing a little, she was keenly aware of how tightly Wyatt was holding her. Her head was dizzy again, but it had nothing to do with cracking it against the wall.

"I still feel bad you got hurt."

Gabby leaned back and smiled. "It's just a bump on the head."

Cupping her cheek, he rubbed his thumb across her cheek. "I think it would break my heart if something happened to you. No, I know it would."

What was going on with him? He'd kissed her when they'd returned from Lubbock, and they'd had little interaction since then. "Really, I'm fine."

"If I ask you something, will you be honest?" He dropped his hand from her face and sat back a little, his gaze continuing to bore through her.

She knitted her eyebrows together. Wyatt was acting so strangely. "As honest as I know how to be."

"Are you and Bandit serious?" He held her gaze. "Like, really serious?"

She didn't know how to respond. Did she 'fess up and tell him it had been a lie? What then? If she told him the truth, he'd want to know why, and she wasn't sure she could tell him. "Well..."

The word was barely spoken before he brought his lips down to hers. Was this his form of truth serum? If so, it had an excellent chance of working. His arms wrapped around her, pulling her flush to him.

With the second brush of his lips against hers, her lips parted, and he deepened the kiss. She slid her hands up his chest and around his neck, her fingers stretching into his hair. This kiss was nothing like the one they'd shared in the truck. It was hard and demanding, making her heart quicken with every second that passed.

He broke the kiss, trailing feathery open-mouth kisses from her lips to her collarbone, across the sensitive skin of her neck, to just below her ear where he stopped. "I've been thinking about kissing you since we came back from Lubbock."

Blood rushed in her ears, making her almost ask him to repeat himself. "You have?"

He leaned back and held her gaze. The intensity was nearly smothering. "I'm a little mixed up as of late."

"Me too," she whispered.

"You and Bandit being together…"

Was that why he'd kissed her? Because he thought she was with Bandit. It sure didn't feel that way. Plus, she knew Wyatt. He'd never hurt Bandit like that. She shook her head. "I'm—"

Carrie Anne charged into Gabby's room. "Hey!"

Startled, Wyatt jumped up and stuffed his hands in his back pockets. "Hey."

"Am I interrupting something?"

Wyatt strode to the door. "Nope, and I'm late meeting the guys. You ladies have fun with your party. Just don't do anything I wouldn't do." The hard look he gave Gabby made her want to crawl under something.

With that, he was gone, and Gabby felt blindsided. Beyond that, her head was beginning to throb.

"What just happened?" Carrie Anne asked.

Gabby blinked. The last thing she wanted to do at the moment was talk about Wyatt or kissing him. Not when her head was pounding. "I ran into him coming up the stairs and hit my head. He was just making sure I was okay."

Her friend approached the bed and sat down. "You hit your head? Should we call a doctor?"

"No, I'm okay. Just some pain medicine, and I'll be good." She pulled her cell phone out of her pocket. "I have less than forty-five minutes to get ready. I need to hurry and get a shower."

"Are you sure? My party isn't worth my best friend being in pain."

Gabby patted Carrie Anne's hand. "I'm fine. Let me get ready."

Carrie Anne gave her a hard look before standing. "Okay, but knowing you have a bump on the head, I'll be watching you like a hawk tonight."

"Okay." Gabby chuckled.

Carrie Anne walked to the door and shut it behind her as she left.

Gabby palmed her forehead and lay back, staring at the ceiling. She knew she had to hurry, but her thoughts were in a whirlwind. Wyatt had kissed her when he thought she was with Bandit. He'd been cheated on, and now he probably felt like he was going behind his friend's back.

If given the opportunity, she'd be setting everything straight with Wyatt. She hoped he didn't hate her forever.

GABBY LEANED her stomach against the counter in front of the sink. Bandit had told her not to worry about the dishes, but unable to sleep, she'd quietly slipped downstairs into the kitchen.

Carrie Anne's party went off without a problem. The conversation was lively, the games were fun, and the food was delicious. Overall, Gabby was pretty pleased with the way things had gone. Mostly, she was happy that Carrie Anne seemed to love it. With as little time as she had to prepare, that was the most important thing to Gabby.

The only dark cloud over her now was Wyatt. Over and over, she'd practiced telling him everything. Each scenario left her in tears and him wishing he'd never see her again. None of them were what she wanted, and if she could go back, she would have never gone along with Carrie Anne's plan.

"You're up late."

Gabby jumped, dropping the glass she was washing, and soapy water splashed onto her shirt. "Wyatt!" She snatched a drying towel and patted down her shirt. "I thought you were in Amarillo for Israel's bachelor party."

He stepped a little farther into the kitchen and

leaned his hip against the island counter. "I was supposed to be, but I had trouble sleeping."

"So you drove home? I didn't even hear you come in."

"I didn't want to wake anyone up."

She braced her hand against the counter and palmed her forehead. Her whole body shook as the adrenaline rushed through her blood. "You scared me to death."

"I didn't mean to, but I'm glad I caught you." His voice held an edge.

She nodded. "I'm glad you did too. I need to tell you something."

Crossing his arms over his chest, he nodded. "That you and Bandit aren't really dating?"

Gabby jerked her head up and looked at Wyatt.

He locked eyes with her, and she nearly withered under the glare. "He told me tonight. After I pleaded for his forgiveness for kissing you."

"Wyatt…"

He dropped his arms and held up his hand. "I don't want to hear it. Not only did you lie to me, but you let me believe I was cheating on my friend. Do you have any idea how guilty I've felt? I thought I had fee—" He cut himself short of finishing the sentence, looking disgusted with himself.

What could she say? That it was Carrie Anne's idea? That didn't make it any better. It didn't change that Gabby had gone along with it. There was no amount of excuses that could make any of what she'd done okay. "I know, and I'm sorry. I was waiting for you to get back to tell you the truth."

"Why did you do it?" His voice broke, and along with it, the last shred of her heart.

"I thought if you believed I was unavailable, you'd see me differently. I thought...it'd make you..." Now that she was saying it aloud, it was stupid. Games and tricks and deceit weren't how you started relationships. If she'd just been honest from the beginning, he may not have seen her as someone he wanted to date, but at least he wouldn't be looking at her like she'd gutted him.

He crossed the room and stopped in front of her, piercing her with a look. "Those kisses we shared meant nothing to me. I'd thought about giving up the rodeo to move home. I was going to do it for—" He stopped short. "It doesn't matter. You lied to me. Played me for a fool. I won't do anything to hurt our families, but you should stay away from me from now on. You're right. Those five years you were away, you did change. Just not for the better."

Gabby fought to hold back tears as each venom-coated dagger hit. He had every right to be angry. "I know."

Wyatt turned and walked out of the kitchen. As soon as he was out of sight, Gabby lost the fight, and tears streamed down her cheeks. A soft sob escaped and then another until she slid to the floor, covering her face with her hands. She'd made such a mess of things. And she couldn't see how it would ever be fixed.

CHAPTER 21

"What are you doing in here?" asked Bear. "Still upset about Gabby?"

Wyatt looked up from where he sat by the window in the study. "No, I just wanted a minute to myself. I hadn't checked out this area of the house yet and thought I'd give it a try."

More like he couldn't stand being in the same room with Gabby. Not that he'd kept tabs of where she was. He'd done his best to ignore even caring if she was around. He'd finally decided to come clean to Bandit after feeling terrible for so long, and finding out from Bandit that she'd lied to him had made him sick to his stomach. Wyatt hadn't even given Bandit a chance to respond before he'd marched out of the hotel and took off in his truck. He'd driven around

Amarillo a little while and ignored the more than dozen phone calls from his brothers and Carrie Anne. He'd not been in the mood to chat.

It didn't matter to Wyatt why she'd done it. It only mattered that she had, and now the very sight of her made him wish she'd stayed in Charleston. He'd been so close to telling her…he pushed the thought away. Whatever feelings he might have had were gone now.

Lunch had been a few hours ago. Wyatt had found himself needing a minute to think without all the noise and found this room to be perfect for a man with much on his mind.

It wasn't stuffy, but it was well-decorated. He could see little touches that he was sure Bear had a hand in. Dark wood bookcases lined the wall, with a desk to match. A set of chairs faced the window with a small table between them, and a few decanters sat on a buffet-style table that looked like it was an antique.

Bear crossed the room and took a seat in the other chair. "I like the study being away from the living room. I had the contractor give it a little extra sound-proofing. It's quiet, and I figured once the place is actually functioning as a working ranch again, I'll need it."

"I'm sure you will." Wyatt set his ankle over his knee. "I'd like to talk to you about the orchard."

"The orchard? Won't you be going back on tour with the rodeo?"

Shaking his head, Wyatt let out a long breath. He'd gone back and forth about the orchard, trying to decide if he still wanted it. Then he'd come to the conclusion that he wasn't going to let the ties to Gabby keep him from doing something he wanted. "No, I'm going to do one more ride to finish my eight seconds, and then I'll hang up my saddle."

Bear's jaw hung open. "I never thought I'd hear those words come from your mouth."

"Me either, but I want more out of life. I had fun with it when I was a kid, and I enjoyed the crowds and all that. Lately, I haven't enjoyed it." He'd figured that out over the last few days. Even if he was staying on the entire eight seconds and giving it his all, he still wasn't satisfied.

"I thought you loved it."

"I did, but I want more than eight seconds of glory. I want to build a life and a future. Something that I can pass down to my kids, something I can be proud of. I'm not knocking riders or the rodeo, but it's just not what I want anymore."

Bear rubbed his jaw with his knuckles. "Well, if your heart isn't in it, then I agree."

Wyatt smiled. "It's not, and I'd like to purchase that orchard from you."

"Aw, man, it's yours. You can have it. I've got plenty of acreage."

He figured his brother would say that. The only thing the money had changed for Bear so far was his address. Everything else about him was just as simple as it was before. "I know, but I want something that's mine. Something I can share with someone."

Shrugging, Bear said, "All right. I think we can do that. It'll need to be after the holiday. I might be a billionaire, but I'm blue-collar smart. The holiday rate would be astronomical."

Wyatt held his stomach as he belly-laughed. "I bet it would be."

"What are your plans for the place?"

This part was what had kept Wyatt up the last few nights. It gave him an excitement about the future bull riding had never given him. But it also weighed on him because he'd hoped Gabby would be a part of it. He'd gone back and forth about whether he could go on with the plans without her. He'd been so close to telling her how he felt about her. After being so blind all those years, he hadn't wanted her to have any doubts that he cared about her. But now none of that mattered. He hadn't even had one real chance with her, and it was hard to let the dream go. He could do it, though.

As the sun gradually sank behind the horizon, Wyatt talked over his plans with Bear. During the talk, one by one, his brothers and then their dad joined them. It was an animated discussion about all aspects of it. The biggest issue was the house. Could it be salvaged? His dad seemed to think it could. Hunter disagreed. Wyatt hoped his dad was right, but he suspected Hunter knew what he was talking about since he was a house flipper.

He didn't need Gabby to make that orchard more than just a house with some trees. All he needed was a healthy budget and time. Eventually, he'd see it as a home, and who knew, maybe he'd find someone to share his dreams with who wasn't a liar.

His heart felt skewered with the very idea of someone besides Gabby standing hand in hand with him, making that plot of land a home. He forcefully shut the thoughts down. She'd lied. And once a liar, always a liar. He didn't need that. What he needed was to move on. Something bigger and better was in store for him.

As Wyatt stepped out of his truck, the front door of the house opened. Carrie Anne stomped down the steps, pointing to the barn. "You. Me. Barn. Now!" By the looks of her, he was about to get the chewing of a lifetime.

"Why?" He'd just gotten back from looking at the orchard again. It was cold, and he'd planned on warming up with some coffee.

"We need to talk and now."

"If it's about Gabby, I don't want to talk."

His sister stopped inches from him and glared up at him. "Tough. We're talking."

He stepped back. "Carrie Anne, I'm in no mood to deal with you. She lied. End of story."

"It was my idea."

His sister's idea? Gabby never said that. Whatever. "I don't care. I still don't want to talk."

As he went to go around her, she caught him by the arm and stopped him. "You've broken her, Wyatt."

"Good! She deserves it." Even as he said it, his chest constricted. He knew he'd been angry, but his sister didn't use words like that just because.

"And this was my fault. I was the one who planned the whole thing. She's loved you since she knew what the word meant. When was the first time it hit you that she wasn't family or friend? Right after you saw her with Bandit?"

Wyatt set his hands on his hips, turned his back on her, and swore under his breath. That was true. He'd started seeing her different at the airport, but he'd never allowed himself to think of her as anything other than Carrie Anne's best friend until Bandit was in the picture. He turned and faced his sister. "So what? She didn't have to lie."

Carrie Anne's entire body sagged. "Wyatt, it was all my fault. If you're going to hold on to hate for someone, it should be me." She rubbed her arms. "Can we please talk in the barn? This wind has a bite."

"Fine."

They walked to the barn, and once they were both inside, he shut the door.

Carrie Anne walked to one of the stalls and leaned back against the gate. Silence stretched as the wind screeched outside and currents pushed loose hay across the dirt floor.

"If you're going to talk, talk. Otherwise, I have things to do," he said.

"Have you noticed she hasn't been around?"

"She's missed a few meals. It's not that big of a deal."

"A few? Try since after my bachelorette party three

days ago. She hasn't been out of her room. I've seen her once, and tomorrow is Christmas Eve. Wyatt, she's in shreds. I think the only reason she's still here is because she won't leave me before the wedding."

When he didn't respond, she continued. "It was me. She didn't want to go along with it, but I talked her into it. This whole thing is on me."

He huffed. "Why would you do that?"

Carrie Anne took a few steps toward him. "Because you are the densest person I know, and I thought it would be a good idea to make you jealous. To be honest, I think it worked. Otherwise, you wouldn't be this angry."

"Then I'm mad at both of you." He turned his back on her.

"I didn't know what else to do. Something had to get your attention before it was too late." Carrie Anne's posture softened. "You've always gone to her when you were upset or troubled. You've always managed to put yourself next to her. Every camping trip we went on, there you were, with Gabby."

"Because she was my friend." Except, friends didn't share hot kisses...three kisses. The first could be... explained away, maybe. But the others? Webster's was devoid of words that could come close to how that felt.

Carrie Anne stared at him in disbelief. "And isn't that what a relationship is supposed to be? To be best friends, loving each other until their last breath? Israel is my best friend. If I'm hurt, I find him. If I'm troubled, I find him. He's the first person I want for everything."

She took Wyatt by the shoulders and locked eyes with him. "You say right here and now that you don't care for her that way, and I will walk away. I'll let Gabby cry on my shoulder, tell her she can do better because that's what a good friend does, and help her get over you."

"I—"

"Be honest. With me. With yourself. If not for yourself, for Gabby. Why *are* you angry? If she's just family, does it really matter?"

"I don't like being lied to. Isn't that reason enough?"

She walked around him and made him face her. "Now who's the liar?"

"I'm not—"

"Really?

He walked to the upturned bucket and took a seat, raking his hand through his hair. "This entire time, guilt has been eating me alive because I was having feelings for another guy's girl. That was a rotten thing to do. This isn't me. I don't go around stealing another man's girlfriend."

"Guilty about what?"

"I kissed her. Three times." He looked up. "But she kissed me back every time. I was a horrible person because I'd kissed her, only to find out…it wasn't true. I felt like a fool."

"Did she tell you she was dating Bandit? Did those exact words fall from her lips?"

Wyatt shook his head. "No, but they were hanging all over each other."

Carrie Anne scoffed. "So, then you've dated all those rodeo girls that hung all over you?"

"That's different. I didn't know them."

"There's zero difference. If you aren't dating Gabby, she's free to hang on anyone she wants. The problem is, you didn't want her dating anyone."

He hung his head and closed his eyes. There was no more point in fighting it. His sister was right. "Ever since I picked her up at the airport, things have been different. Our whole past is different. All those times I'd make sure my sleeping bag was next to hers. That year she wore the red dress and I wanted to punch the guy who was taking her to prom. Proposing to Lori when I heard Gabby talking about moving to Charleston. I think I've been fighting tooth and nail against the truth because I couldn't get past the fact that she was family." He paused. "And then that day at the orchard when I wanted to kiss her so bad it hurt, I... the truth was, I did have feelings for her."

Carrie Anne closed the distance and squatted in front of him. "Wyatt, tell the truth. Are you really angry, or are you scared?"

Wyatt pulled away, took his hat off, and slapped it against his leg. "Geez, Carrie Anne, it's not that simple. If something happens and it doesn't work…"

Carrie Anne pinched her lips together. "You sell that snake oil elsewhere and tell the truth. You're more scared of Gabby than you are of a bull."

Scared? He wasn't scared. That was ridiculous. "I'm…not."

She let out a soft breath. "You're afraid of falling in love."

"I'm afraid of hurting her!" he blurted before he even realized he'd had the thought.

His sister stood as she grinned. "And there it is."

Wyatt came off his seat. "I don't want to hurt her. I don't want to lose what we have if it goes south. I can't picture life without her. I think I'd wither and die."

"You *are* hurting her, and you're going to hurt her again."

He turned to face her. "Well, thanks, sis."

"And she's going to hurt you. It's life. And it isn't about how much you hurt each other. It's about what you do when you realize you've hurt each other. Do you walk away, or do you make it right? It's loving and laughing and fighting and being strong enough to bend when you need to. It's compromise and forgiveness and grace." Carrie Anne smiled. "It's a partnership all the way to your soul."

"What if I make a mistake?"

"That's an inevitable part of loving someone."

His stomach churned as he thought back to the night of the bachelorette party. "I hurt her, Carrie Anne. I told her she meant nothing to me. I don't think she'll ever forgive me."

Carrie Anne's head dropped back. "Oh, Wyatt."

"I was just going to talk to her, and the more I drove around, the angrier I got. By the time I got back home, I couldn't see straight."

His sister rolled her lips in and cringed. "Oh, Wyatt. If she loves you like I know she loves you, I think you can go in there and apologize. I'm not saying that will fix all of it, but it'll be a start."

"I've fallen for her. I don't know what I'll do if she doesn't forgive me."

"I think she will. I just don't think it'll be easy." She hooked her arm through his. "Let's go inside. I need a fire to thaw out my bones. I'm freezing in here."

Wyatt was freezing all right, but it had nothing to do with the weather. He'd been mean and cruel and hateful to Gabby. It would be a flat-out miracle if she forgave him. He'd have to find a way to apologize that she couldn't run from.

He quickly looked up and inwardly begged for mercy. He wanted her, to be with her, and he hoped she still wanted him. If she did, he'd spend the rest of his life grateful he fell in love with a woman patient enough to put up with him.

"You think she'll listen?" he whispered as they walked through the barn.

Carrie Anne squeezed his arm. "She's loved you for forever. I know she will."

He held Carrie Anne's gaze a moment, debating how he should tell Gabby. Should it be simple? Should it be something so grand there'd be no doubt in her mind how he felt about her? There was a rodeo coming to Amarillo the day after Christmas. He hadn't planned on participating, but it could be his last ride. A good ride.

If Gabby was there, he knew he could stay on those eight seconds, and then he could tell her. He could retire and tell her he was ready to start a life with her, and there'd be no doubt that he was sorry. He wanted to live out the dream they'd had since they were teenagers. A new, better dream. One that had her by his side and at the center of his world.

Carrie rolled her eyes. "Don't overthink this. Just tell her."

"What if she thinks I'm only saying it because—"

"She won't."

Wyatt shook his head. "No, I want to wait. There's a rodeo event coming to Amarillo between Christmas and New Year's Eve. It's just a small one, but I could tell her after my ride. My full ride."

Carrie Anne jerked to a stop and put her hands on her hips. "Right before my wedding? No way."

"It'll be fine. I'll be fine."

Carrie Anne crossed her arms over her chest and shook her head. "If you get hurt…"

He gave her a crooked grin. "I've only been hurt once. I've got the best reason in the world to stay on this time. The whole family can be there. I can tell everyone that I choose her because I want her. I can tell her then, and she'll know for sure it's the absolute truth. That I love her—"

The words made him come to a full stop. He loved her. He'd always loved her. Now that it was out, he felt light and free. It was the truest thing he'd ever felt.

His sister grinned wide. "I knew you loved her."

"I do. I do love her with all my heart."

"Well, it only took a sledgehammer, but that thick head of yours finally got it."

Laughing, Wyatt shook his head. "Okay, fine. I deserve that."

Dropping her arms to her side, she said, "I still don't like you riding right before my wedding."

"If I get a weird feeling, I won't. But I'll still tell Gabby."

Silence stretched as Carrie Anne seemed to consider what he'd said. "All right." She hooked her arm through his again. "Let's go. The fire's calling my name."

Wyatt nodded. He wasn't cold. His insides were blazing. He was picturing himself riding a full eight seconds, dismounting, and then telling the world he loved Gabby Fredericks. He just knew that would be the best way: walking away from the rodeo when he'd conquered his fear and then facing his future with the one person he loved most in the world.

A smile stretched wide on his lips as he thought about the new future he was planning. The one where he and Gabby faced the world together.

CHAPTER 22

*N*ormally, Christmas Eve was Gabby's favorite part of the holidays. Bandit's cinnamon rolls and time with family. Before the Wests won the lottery, everyone would be squished into her parents' house or the Wests's home. It was warm and cozy and familiar. All the things that made Christmas great.

This year was such a stark contrast. There were no elbows to the ribs or sitting on the floor. No *excuse me, can I slide by you?* Cups filled with drinks were safe from spills because there wasn't a gauntlet of people to get around. All the annoying things that made it... Christmas with family.

Instead, there was a trimmed twelve-foot tree so perfect it looked fake and sofas in a half-moon around it. Everyone had a spot to sit. It was comfortable and spacious. Gabby almost missed the annual meeting of the sardines decking the halls.

Stephanie moaned as she picked up the last bite of her cinnamon roll and popped it in her mouth. She melted, and her eyes crossed. "Oh, hot and gooey and sweet. How I have missed you, cinna-friend."

"I think this is the part I love most about Christmas Eve." Chuckling, Gabby stabbed her fork into the cinnamon roll and pulled off a bite. "They get better every year."

Finishing her bite, Stephanie took a sip of milk. "I know. I think it's what gets me through the year." She laughed. "That boyfriend of yours can sure cook." It was a little louder than necessary, and a few people looked their way. One of them being Wyatt.

Gabby glared at her. "Bandit can definitely cook."

"I haven't had nearly the fun I thought I would by now," Stephanie whispered.

"Stop that."

"I don't know why you don't just tell him how you feel. You can tell he feels the same way about you."

How Gabby wished that were true, but he'd made himself loud and clear that night of the bachelor party. Since then, she'd tried to stay out of his way. He had a right to hate her, and she wasn't about to fault him for it.

A little more than twenty-four hours ago, she'd pulled herself together enough to stop crying. For too long, she'd held a roman candle for a man who wasn't meant to be hers and never would be now. It had hurt worse than a scorpion sting, but once the initial burn had worn off, she was okay. Not great. Not fantastic, but okay.

There were a couple of times Wyatt had tried to talk to her, but she'd tucked tail and run. Her heart still had shrapnel lodged in it, and she'd needed a minute to find all the pieces.

She'd spent her time making plans for her future, spending time looking into loans so she could purchase the paper. Now that Wyatt hated her, he'd probably go back to the rodeo instead of pursuing the orchard. Not that she could blame him. She wouldn't want to spend time in a place that reminded her of someone who hurt her.

Stephanie tapped her on the arm. "Hey, this is for you."

Gabby startled, wiped her mouth with a napkin, and took the small present from her sister. She put it up to her ear and shook it. Whatever it was, it was light and didn't make much noise. She looked at it again and found that her name was the only name on the tag. "Who is this from?"

Everyone looked around at each other. Her mom finally spoke up. "I have no idea. I picked it because it was the smallest gift."

Another part of their Christmas Eve tradition was that they couldn't pick their own "smallest" gift. That had started roughly twenty years ago when Josiah tried to cheat and open one of his bigger gifts.

"Okay, confess. Who is this from?" Gabby asked as her gaze roamed from face to face.

Hunter chuckled. "Just open it."

Gabby grumbled under her breath. "Fine," she said and peeled the paper off to reveal a small white box. She lifted the lid and sighed as she pulled a sprig of mistletoe out. Her heart ached for a split-second, thinking it might be from Wyatt. "Funny."

"It's from me." Stephanie snatched the sprig from her, jumped out of her chair, and ran to the entryway of the kitchen. "Okay, you guys be careful. There's mistletoe now." She wiggled her eyebrows at Gabby and then Bandit.

Hanging her head, Gabby groaned. Just what she needed. "Stephanie. Get that down." She glanced over her shoulder. "Please."

"No way. This will be fun." She winked.

Translation: Her sister had turned up the fun knob to eleven. She probably wouldn't have if Gabby had told her what happened, but so far, she'd lacked the courage to tell anyone. She'd barely even spoken to Carrie Anne.

Stephanie returned to her seat and grinned. "You'll love it."

"I already hate it."

Hunter laughed. "I don't know. Could be fun for someone."

After everyone had finished opening their one gift, they talked a little longer before Josiah and Mr. West suggested a card game.

"Nope, I'm having some hot tea and working on this puzzle I just got," Mrs. West said. "How about you?" She looked at Gabby's mom. "Want to join me? I bet we can put the puzzle together before they're done with the game."

Laughing, Gabby's mom nodded. "I could go for some hot tea and a puzzle as well. Who else wants to join us?"

Card game or puzzles? Gabby finished off her cinnamon roll and stood.

Stephanie touched her arm. "Where are you going?"

Gabby smiled. "I'm putting my dishes up and going

to bed."

"It's only nine," Wyatt said.

Without looking his direction, she said, "I'm tired."

"Wait!" Wyatt called out. "I need to make an announcement."

Gabby paused, and everyone stopped what they were doing to look at him.

"There's a small rodeo coming to Amarillo the day after Christmas. I wasn't going to participate at first, but they allowed me to register late. I'll be riding. I wanted to see if everyone wanted to go."

Mrs. West's mouth dropped open. "Have you lost your mind? That's right before Carrie Anne's wedding."

His eyes widened as if he wasn't expecting her to object. "Mom, I cleared it with her first."

"And I said I didn't like it." Carrie Anne waggled her finger at him.

Mr. West made a time-out signal with his hands. "Whoa, nellies. Now, Wyatt, your momma has a good point."

Wyatt's mom pointed her finger at Wyatt. "See—"

His dad held up his hand. "But Wyatt is a good rider. Out of all the rides he's done, he's had one accident. Granted, it was a big one, but that's it. Course, he's had bruises in places it's not polite to talk about in mixed company, but I think he'll be okay."

Mrs. West shook her head. "I don't like it. If he gets hurt..."

"I won't. If I have a bad feeling about it at all, I won't ride. I promise."

With his attention on his parents, Gabby slipped off to the kitchen. She was pretty sure she wasn't on the guest list. The metal sink clinked as she set her dishes down, and the fork she'd used clattered as it fell off her plate. She turned, and Wyatt was standing in the kitchen doorway.

"Are you really that tired?" he asked.

She looked down and nodded. "Yeah."

The sound of footsteps drawing closer made her lift her head. Wyatt was now directly in front of her. "I wanted—"

Holding up her hand, she stopped him. "I know. It's okay. I messed things up, and I don't expect them to ever be where they were. Not after lying to you."

"Gabby, just let me—"

"No." She pinched the bridge of her nose and then lifted her gaze to his again. "You need time, and I need time. Let's just call it a truce for a while. Please?"

He sighed. "All right, but I want you at my event. Okay?"

"All right," she said softly.

He shot her a sweet half-grin and walked back to the kitchen doorway. "See you in the morning."

Well, at least he didn't hate her guts as much as she thought he did. Maybe there was a chance they could be normal again. She wouldn't hold her breath or get her hopes up, but this was a start.

CHAPTER 23

*H*eart palpitations. Sweaty palms. Upset stomach. Wyatt's anxiety ratcheted up with every second his ride drew closer. Whispers he'd heard about the bull he'd drawn was that it was mean as a snake. He was the biggest bull at the event, and if he got you off the saddle, he was coming for you.

Wyatt's gut feeling was that he'd be okay, but that didn't mean he was stupid enough to believe the ride would be easy. He was going to have to keep his mind focused. When he dismounted, he was going to need to bolt out of the arena as fast as possible.

He shook his hands out as he paced, psyching himself up. As he turned, he looked over the crowd, trying to find his family. More importantly, he wanted to see Gabby. This was for her as much as it was for him.

Wyatt sensed someone watching, whirled around, and smiled as his gaze landed on Gabby. "Hey."

She hooked a thumb over her shoulder. "I'm sorry. I'll go."

He quickly closed the distance. "No, wait. I'm glad you're here. I wish you'd come to see me like this at every event you came to." He gave her a small smile.

Her brows furrowed in confusion. "I saw you pacing...and just...wanted to make sure you were okay." She slid her hands into her back jeans pockets and shrugged.

"Yeah, just...pre-ride jitters. You know how it is." Now that she was standing in front of him, he wasn't nervous at all. "Getting myself ready to go out there."

"You do know if you get hurt, Carrie Anne will make you wish the bull had killed you." She rolled her lips in to keep from smiling.

Wyatt cast his gaze to the ground and grinned as he shook his head. "Oh, I bet she will, but I'm going to walk out of that arena." More like leave it for something he wanted more than anything. He took Gabby's hand. "Thanks for checking on me."

The corners of her lips turned up a fraction. "I don't want you to get hurt either."

He loved hearing that. He stepped closer to her. "You think I could get a kiss for good luck?"

Gabby locked eyes with him like she was looking for a miracle. "You think you'll ever be able to really forgive me?"

"How about that kiss for good luck, and we'll start negotiations there?"

She tilted her head, eyebrows drawn together like she was trying to figure out what he was doing. "Okay." Lifting slightly on her toes, she kissed his cheek. "You don't need luck. You're going to be great."

He smiled and turned. As he got to the chute, he paused. If he was going into that arena with a two-ton bull, he wanted to make sure he at least got one more of her kisses, just in case.

He wrapped one arm around her waist, held the nape of her neck with the other, and touched his lips to hers.

Just as they touched, the announcer called his name. The crowd cheered and the noise nearly deafened him. Man, his timing smelled to high heaven, but a quick kiss was better than nothing.

When he pulled back, he said, "I'm riding for you."

"What?"

"After this, I'm done. This is my last ride. If something bad happens, I need you to know that I love you."

Her mouth dropped open, and her eyes widened.

"Talk later." He winked and jogged back to the bullpen, climbed up the side, and hopped onto the bull. He had a lot more to say, but it would be after. Hopefully, he'd get the answer he wanted when it was all said and done.

CHAPTER 24

a cheering crowd, a buzzer loud enough to give her hearing loss, and what had Wyatt just said? This was his last ride? More importantly, he loved her? She quickly pinched herself. This was a weird dream. It had to be.

Surely Gabby had heard Wyatt wrong. Maybe he loved her as a friend, but that was all it could be. He was still angry at her for lying to him.

She should have said no to the kiss. Apparently, her iron will was a little more aluminum than actual iron. He'd asked, looking at her with those puppy dog eyes, and her head had bobbled like a doll. It didn't help that he was in jeans and chaps, looking like a star in a Western.

Love? He said he loved her? No way. She had to be

hearing things. It was what she'd wanted for years, but there was no way that was true. What was he doing to her? More importantly, why was he doing it?

The buzzer rang, the gate opened, and the bull shot out. She ran to the nearest stand and pulled herself onto it so she could watch. In all her years going to events, she'd never seen a bigger bull. The thing was a monster, and it was bucking like its only life purpose was to get Wyatt off. She also got the feeling that if it did manage to get Wyatt off, it would do its best to stomp him into the ground.

Normally, eight seconds wasn't all that long, but watching Wyatt hang on made those seconds tick by in slow motion. It would only take one mistake, and he could be hurt. The last three seconds showed on the time clock, and she took a deep breath, holding it as she silently counted down.

When the timer hit zero, she screamed and clapped along with the entire crowd. It was a great ride. Now, all he had to do was get off the bull and get to safety.

Again, she held her breath as Wyatt unwrapped his hand and dismounted. The bull zeroed in on him, and Wyatt ran for the closest way out. He had hardly made it out before that giant bull rammed into the gate.

This time, Gabby let out the breath she'd been holding and said a quick prayer of thanks. She jumped down from the bleachers and found her way back to where the rest of the family was sitting.

"Gabby!" Wyatt called.

She paused at the edge of the bleachers and turned to face him. What was he doing?

"I said we'd start negotiations!" He ran toward her and stopped.

"What?"

"I have something to say to you, Gabrielle Fredericks."

"Okay." She looked around.

Suddenly, the crowd grew quiet as they noticed something was going on, and a spotlight swung around, planting them right in the middle of it. "What's going on?"

"It's recently come to my attention that I am a thick-headed, stupid man. I've had the best thing in my life staring me right in the face, and I've been too blind to see it." He shot her a smile. "I'm here to rectify that."

"What?"

He took a step closer. "You. It's always been you. You've always been the best thing, and you've been right in front of my face all along."

Gabby blinked. Her heart pounded in her chest so hard she had to focus on what he was saying. This couldn't possibly be happening. He'd said that their kisses hadn't meant anything. That he was done with her. "What?"

He took her hand and placed it over his heart. "I'm in love with you. It took far too long to get wise enough to see it, but I'm wholly aware now that you are all I want. I love you, Gabby Fredericks."

"What?" The three little words she'd hoped for had come from his lips, but she was almost too stunned to take them in.

Wyatt dipped his head and chuckled. "Can you please say something other than 'what'?"

She opened and closed her mouth a few times, trying to make sense of what was going on. "You love me?"

He slid his arm around her back and pulled her closer as he nodded. "With all my heart. Forever and always. This was my last ride, and I'd like to start a new ride with you."

"But...you were so angry..."

"Because at the time, I didn't know my sister was the mastermind behind the whole scheme to make me jealous." He grinned. "And I'm glad she did it. I wasn't angry with you. I was angry because I had feelings for you, and I was afraid. I'm hoping I'm not too late. You think you can forgive me for being so stupid?"

Tears pricked her eyes as she smiled. "I don't know. You were pretty stupid," she said, laughing as tears streaked down her cheeks.

"I can't deny that." He smiled. "Will you let me love you to make up for it? I promise I won't be that stupid ever again."

"I think that'll work. I'll make sure you aren't, even if I have to spell everything out."

The crowd roared as he brought his lips down to hers. She circled her arms around his neck, and it seemed as if the noise of the crowd grew louder than before. They broke the kiss, and he touched his forehead to hers. "I love you."

"I love you, too."

The three words she'd waited a lifetime for, dreamed of hearing—and not a single dream came close to how they sounded coming from his lips. He loved her.

EPILOGUE

New Year's Eve...

Carrie Anne's wedding day had one little bump. The family had scrambled to find large tents when a snowstorm unexpectedly popped up on the radar. It had dumped six inches the night before, and Wyatt's baby sister was beside herself.

Josiah had come to the rescue big time. A client of his who had purchased commercial property happened to own a rental shop. He'd put in a call, and the company had them driven from Dallas that next morning with just enough time for the ceremony to start.

Wyatt, Bear, and Josiah had taken on the task of clearing the snow so the guests wouldn't be walking in cold wet sludge before the affair was over. It had taken quick work and a lot of shoveling, but they'd managed to clear it in time to get the tents up.

The actual ceremony, however, was nice. It was simple, which Wyatt liked. They'd all worn tuxes with little purple peonies pinned on the lapel. The brides-maids, all five of them, wore knee-length purple dresses to match. There was the exchange of vows with Carrie Anne bawling like a baby, and Wyatt was pretty sure Israel had shed a few tears.

His favorite part was when he was able to loosen his tie. If he didn't know any better, his brother had been trying to choke him. That thing was so tight that a few times he wondered if his head wasn't turning beet red. If he took nothing else away from this wedding, it was that Bear was never touching his ties again.

Carrie Anne sidled up next to him as guests danced on the dance floor. "It's less than an hour until the new year. Got any resolutions?"

He cut a glance at her. "Maybe."

"I hope you've adopted a smarter, swifter way of life."

"Hush. I'll mess up your hair."

She popped him on the arm. "You do, and I'll have

a posse on you so fast you'll wish you hadn't. This is four hours of work."

"Four hours? What did they use? Curlers harvested from the tips of Mount Everest?"

"No, and shut up."

His shoulders bounced as he laughed. "I'm just messing with you. You're so pretty you made your husband cry."

"Now was that so hard?"

"I think I died a little inside."

She huffed and leaned in. "Don't you waste another minute of time, Wyatt West. You got me?"

He knew exactly what she meant, and now that he had her blessing, he knew exactly what he was going to do. Winding through the crowd, he found Gabby to Hunter.

Gabby turned to Wyatt. "Hey."

"Would you like to dance?"

"I'd love to."

When they reached the dance floor, he slid his arm around her waist and held her close. "I've been thinking a lot about the new year."

"Yeah, I bet you have. Retiring from bull riding is a big deal."

"Nah, not about that." He chuckled. "You and me."

"Us?"

"I'm buying the orchard from Bear. We've been working out the details, and as soon as the world goes back to business, we're making it official."

She gasped. "Really?"

"Yeah, but it's missing a piece. A really crucial part of the whole thing."

"What? Did you find out something was wrong?"

Wyatt shook his head. "No." He went down to one knee. "You're the crucial part. I don't want the orchard without you. I'd really like it to be our home; our venture; our blood, sweat, and tears mingled together. It's not home without you."

Gabby touched her fingers to her mouth. "Wyatt."

"Say yes. Please say yes. You're my best friend, and you're the only best friend I want. Now and forever." He pulled out the small box he'd hidden in his tux and flipped it open. "Will you please marry me?"

She gasped and nodded as tears ran down her cheeks. "Yes."

He slipped the ring on her finger, stood, and grabbed her by the waist, swinging her around. "Yes!"

The guests clapped and hollered.

"It's about time," Bear called out.

Wyatt set Gabby down and held her tight. "I love you."

"I love you."

He touched his lips to hers as fireworks blasted behind them. His new year was already starting better than any other year. He had Gabby and a plan for more than eight seconds.

For a list of all books by Bree Livingston, please visit her website at www.breelivingston.com.

ABOUT THE AUTHOR

Bree Livingston lives in the West Texas Panhandle with her husband, children, and cats. She'd have a dog, but they took a vote and the cats won. Not in numbers, but attitude. They wouldn't even debate. They just leveled their little beady eyes at her and that was all it took for her to nix getting a dog. Her hobbies include...nothing because she writes all the time.

She loves carbs, but the love ends there. No, that's not true. The love usually winds up on her hips which is why she loves writing romance. The love in the pages of her books are sweet and clean, and they definitely don't add pounds when you step on the scale. Unless of course, you're actually holding a Kindle while you're weighing. Put the Kindle down and try again. Also, the cookie because that could be the problem too. She knows from experience.

Join her mailing list to be the first to find out

publishing news, contests, and more by going to her website at https://www.breelivingston.com.

facebook.com/BreeLivingstonWrites

twitter.com/BreeLivWrites

bookbub.com/authors/bree-livingston

Made in the USA
Coppell, TX
01 June 2020